Abruptly Tariq stood. Samira blinked, her gaze sliding over his amazing bronzed body.

Surely it wasn't regret she felt because he was leaving?

Recognising that she didn't want him to leave stole her voice.

'That's a start,' he murmured finally.

'A start?'

Tariq nodded. 'One day soon we'll be husband and wife in every sense of the word.'

Samira shook her head. He had it all wrong.

'Not because I demand it but because it's what we both want.' He leaned close, his eyes tourmaline shards that dared her to deny it. 'I promise you, Samira, you'll be with me every step of the way.'

It was a threat but it sounded like a promise. A promise that sounded appallingly enticing. She wanted to object, argue, say something to puncture his arrogant certainty. But instead her tongue cleaved to the roof of her mouth.

His gaze scorched and Samira felt the sizzle in every inch of her body. His slow smile hitched his mouth up at one side, creating a sexy groove down one cheek that made her insides clutch. He looked so utterly confident—as if he'd never had a doubt in his life.

'The next time you kiss me it won't be because I ask, Samira, but because you want me.'

DESERT VOWS

Two powerful desert princes…
and the only women who can tame them

Sultan Asim of Jazeer and Sheikh Tariq of Al-Sarath
are both bound by honour, duty and tradition. They've
always known they must marry, but it will be for the
good of their kingdoms—*not* for love. Yet now two
very different women threaten the vows Asim and
Tariq have always sworn to uphold.

As desire burns hotter than the desert sand can these
powerful men withstand the heat of temptation?

Find out in:

THE SULTAN'S HAREM BRIDE
February 2015

THE SHEIKH'S PRINCESS BRIDE
April 2015

THE SHEIKH'S PRINCESS BRIDE

BY
ANNIE WEST

First published in Great Britain 2015
by Mills & Boon, an imprint of Harlequin (UK) Limited,
Eton House, 18-24 Paradise Road, Richmond, Surrey, TW9 1SR

ISBN: 978-0-263-25771-7

Harlequin (UK) Limited's policy is to use papers that are natural,
renewable and recyclable products and made from wood grown in
sustainable forests. The logging and manufacturing processes conform
to the legal environmental regulations of the country of origin.

Printed and bound in Great Britain
by CPI Antony Rowe, Chippenham, Wiltshire

Growing up near the beach, **Annie West** spent lots of time observing tall, burnished lifeguards—early research! Now she spends her days fantasising about gorgeous men and their love-lives. Annie has been a reader all her life. She also loves travel, long walks, good company and great food. You can contact her at annie@annie-west.com or via PO Box 1041, Warners Bay, NSW 2282, Australia.

Books by Annie West

Mills & Boon® Modern Romance™

Damaso Claims His Heir
Imprisoned by a Vow
Captive in the Spotlight
Defying Her Desert Duty
Prince of Scandal

Desert Vows

The Sultan's Harem Bride

At His Service

An Enticing Debt to Pay

Dark-Hearted Tycoons

Undone by His Touch

Sinful Desert Nights

Girl in the Bedouin Tent

**Visit the author profile page at
millsandboon.co.uk for more titles**

For Dr G,
the original and the best.
Thank you!

CHAPTER ONE

THE DARK-HAIRED TOTS playing on the far side of the sumptuous hotel lounge held Samira's gaze. They weren't loud
or boisterous, the middle-aged woman with them saw to
that. They were just a pair of ordinary toddlers.

Yet Samira couldn't drag her eyes away from them.
She watched the progress of one little boy as he walked
the length of a sofa, his fingers splayed on the silk uphol-
stery for support. He gurgled his delight and grinned at
his companion who wobbled along behind him.

Samira swallowed. That hollow feeling was back, worse
now, turning into a twisting stab of hurt that knifed all the
way from her womb up high under her ribs.

She tried to focus on Celeste's animated chatter about a
new restaurant. Apparently it had unrivalled rooftop views
of the Eiffel Tower as well as several Michelin stars and
was *the* new place to eat and be seen.

Samira's stomach rebelled at the mention of food.

Or maybe it was something else that made her insides
clench so hard.

The second toddler landed on his bottom, arms wav-
ing, and the woman—grandmother? Nanny?—gathered
him up. Samira's arms twitched then fell, lax and empty,
into her lap.

She blinked and turned away.

Empty. That was exactly how she felt.

She would never have a child of her own to hold. The doctor had made that clear.

She'd tried so hard to regroup these past four years, and she'd come so far, but nothing could erase that searing, hollow ache within.

'I'm so pleased you can attend tonight's charity auction in person.' Celeste leaned across their porcelain teacups and Samira swung her gaze back to the pretty Parisienne. 'Bidders will adore the chance to meet the talented princess behind the gorgeous fashions. Your donation to the auction is sure to fetch a huge price.'

Samira fixed on a practised smile and refused to cringe at yet another reference to her royal status.

As daughter of, and now sister to, the Sultan of Jazeer, she knew all too well that royal rank didn't guarantee happiness.

Her heart lurched but she kept her gaze on her companion, not letting it stray to the other side of the opulent room.

She reminded herself she was a pragmatist. Her successful design business benefited from the cachet of her aristocratic name. Designs by Samira had taken off these last few years. Her clientele, among the globe's ultrawealthy, appreciated working with someone who understood their world, who promised absolute exclusivity and confidentiality. She had far more than many women dreamed of: independence, success, wealth.

What right had she to yearn for more?

Yet still that bone-deep ache persisted, no matter how often she reminded herself how lucky she was. For what did the trappings of success mean when deep at the heart of you there was…nothing?

Samira bit her lip. She *would* conquer this. She would!

'I'm looking forward to it, Celeste.' Samira wrenched her thoughts back to tonight's gala. 'You and your team have done a marvellous job pulling it all together. How, nose, filling lungs that seemed to have cramped shut. 'It sounds like tonight will be a huge success. With luck you'll attract far more than your fund-raising target.'

'Thanks to you.' At Samira's raised brow she shrugged and smiled. 'And to the rest of the donors.' She paused, glancing across the lounge. 'Speak of the devil, there's one of them now.' Celeste sat straighter, swiftly smoothing her short skirt and flicking her blonde hair from her face.

She leaned close to Samira and whispered, 'If only we could auction off a night in his bed we'd make a fortune. I'd bid for that myself and, believe me, I wouldn't let anyone outbid me.'

Surprised at the change in her companion, Samira turned. Yet she knew which man Celeste referred to. It could only be the hunky father of two who wore his elegant clothes with such casual panache that even her long-dormant libido sat up and slavered.

Yet she wasn't prepared for the shock that slammed into her solar plexus as she saw him again. For this time he'd turned and she saw his broad, high brow, defined cheekbones and the rough-cut jaw that looked dangerous and sexy at the same time. A long, harsh blade of a nose somehow melded those too-strong features into a whole that was boldly, outrageously attractive.

And familiar.

Samira's breath hissed sharply as she recognised the man she hadn't seen in years. The man who'd once been almost as dear to her as her brother, Asim.

A tumble of emotions bubbled inside. Excitement and pleasure, regret and pain, and finally a sharp tang of something that tasted like desire, raw and real for the first time in four years. Amazement at that instantaneous response spiralled through her.

'Oh, I'd forgotten you must know him, your country and

his being in the same neighbourhood.' Celeste sounded eager. 'Sexy Sheikh Tariq of Al Sarath.' She sighed gustily. 'I'd even consider taking on a couple of kids for the sake of a man like that. Not that I'll get the chance. They say he hasn't looked at another woman seriously since he lost his wife. They try but none of them last. Apparently he was devoted to her.'

With one final, lingering look at Tariq and his sons, Samira swung round, putting her back to them, letting Celeste's chatter wash over her.

She'd once thought Tariq her friend. She'd looked up to him and trusted him. He'd been as much a part of her life as her brother, Asim. But that friendship had been a mirage, as fragile as the shimmer of water on hot desert sands. He'd turned his back on her years ago with a suddenness that had mystified her, making her wonder what she'd done to alienate him or whether he'd just forgotten her in the press of responsibilities when he'd become Sheikh. When she'd been through hell four years previously she'd not heard a word from him.

Strange how much that still hurt.

Tariq had been in the crowded banqueting hall just three minutes when his sixth sense, the one that always twitched at a hint of trouble, switched into overdrive.

Casually he turned, keenly surveying the glamorous throng even as he returned greetings. He'd been plagued by a sense that something wasn't quite right all afternoon, since he returned to the hotel, but to his annoyance couldn't pinpoint any tangible reason. Just a disturbing sense that he'd missed something important.

It wasn't a sensation he liked. Tariq liked to be in control of his world.

The crowd shifted and through a gap he saw a sliver of deep scarlet. His gaze snagged. Another shift and the scarlet became a long dress, a beacon drawing his eyes to the sultry swell of feminine hips and a deliciously rounded bottom. The woman's skin, displayed by the low scoop of material at her back, was a soft gold, like the desert at first light. A drift of gleaming dark hair was caught up in an artfully casual arrangement that had probably taken hours to achieve. It was worth it, for it revealed the slender perfection of her elegant neck.

Tariq's body tightened, every tendon and muscle stiffening in a response that was profound, instinctive and utterly unexpected.

Light played on the sheen of her dress, lovingly detailing each curve.

He swallowed, realising suddenly that his mouth was dry. His blood flowed hot and fast, his heartbeat tripping to a new, urgent rhythm.

It was a rhythm he hadn't felt in years. Tariq frowned.

The woman turned and he took in the fitted dress that covered her from neck to toe. It enticed a man's imagination to wander over the slim frame and bounteous curves beneath the fabric.

He'd taken half a pace towards her when his eyes lifted to her face and he slammed to a stop, an invisible brick wall smashing into him, tearing the air from his lungs.

Samira.

Tariq heaved in a breath so deep it made his ribs ache.

Samira.

He breathed out, almost tasting the memories on his tongue.

But this wasn't Samira as he'd last seen her. This was a different woman: confident, sexy and experienced. A woman who was making her mark on the world.

For a moment he paused, drawn despite himself. Then his brain kicked into gear as he remembered all the reasons she wasn't for him, despite the tight ache gripping his lower body. He turned to the pretty blonde at his right who was half-wearing a gold sequinned dress. She looked up with wide, hopeful eyes that brimmed with excitement when he smiled down at her.

Minutes later she was leaning into him, her pale hand clutching his sleeve possessively, her eyes issuing an invitation as old as time.

Tariq made himself smile again, wondering if she realised or cared that his attention was elsewhere.

Samira watched him from the back of the crowd. Tariq was the obvious choice of speaker for the children's charity. He was a natural leader, holding the audience in the palm of his hand. Confident, articulate and witty, he effortlessly drew all eyes. Around her men nodded and women salivated and Samira had to repress indignation as they ate him up hungrily.

He was all she remembered: thoughtful, capable and caring, using his speech to reinforce the plight of the children they were here to help, yet keeping the tone just right to loosen the wallets of wealthy patrons.

She remembered a lanky youth who'd always been gentle with her, his friend's little sister. This Tariq was charismatic, with an aura of assured authority that he'd no doubt acquired from ruling his sheikhdom. She couldn't drag her eyes from his tall frame and the way it filled out his tuxedo with solid muscle and bone.

Samira gulped, disorientated at the sudden blast of longing that swamped her.

She blinked and looked up at his bold, handsome face, the glint of humour in his eyes, and remembered the way he'd been with his boys: gentle, loving and patient.

In that moment recognition hit. Recognition of what she wanted.

What she *needed*.

The family she longed for. Children to nurture and love. A partner she could respect and trust to share her life.

Eyes fixed on Tariq, she realised there *was* a way she could become part of a family. It was the perfect solution to her untenable situation. A solution not just for her, but potentially a win-win for all concerned. If she had the courage to pursue it.

The idea was so sudden, so outrageous, she swayed on her delicate heels, her heart thumping high in her throat, her stomach twisting hard and sharp.

'Are you sure you're all right?' Celeste grabbed her elbow as if afraid she'd topple over. 'You weren't yourself this afternoon either.'

'I'm...' Samira gulped, swallowing shock at the revelation confronting her. 'I'm okay, thanks. Just a little tired.'

Celeste nodded and turned back to Tariq. 'He's a little overwhelming, isn't he? Especially in formal dress. I swear, if he wasn't a king someone would snap him up as a model.'

Samira pressed her hand against her churning stomach, only half-listening.

She stared at the powerful figure on the podium and the voice of self-doubt, the voice that had ruled the first twenty-five years of her life, told her she was crazy. Crazy to think about wanting what she could never have. After all, she and Tariq hadn't been friends for years. There was no guarantee he'd even listen to her.

But another part of her applauded. The part that had grown stronger in the last four years, nurtured by her family and her determination to drag herself out of the mire of despair and make something of her life. The voice of the survivor she'd become.

She knew what she wanted.

Why not go for it?

Yet instinctively she shied away from such an action.

That wasn't her style. It never had been. The only time she'd defied convention and upbringing and had reached for what she desired, it had turned to dust and ashes, ruin and grief. She still bore the scars.

Yet what had she to lose by trying? Nothing that mattered when weighed against the possibility of winning what she so desperately craved.

In the mirrored lift, Samira straightened her neat, cinnamon jacket and smoothed her clammy palms down the matching fitted skirt. Her cream blouse was businesslike rather than feminine but this, she reminded herself, was a business meeting.

The most important business meeting of her life.

If only she felt half as confident as at her meetings with clients.

The door hissed open and she stepped out. A few metres took her to the door of the presidential suite and a dark-suited security man.

'Your Highness.' He bowed smoothly and opened the door, admitting her into the suite's luxurious foyer.

Inside, another staff member greeted her.

'If you'd care to take a seat, Your Highness?' He led the way to a beautifully appointed sitting room furnished in shades of soft taupe and aubergine. Large windows offered an unrivalled view of Paris. 'Can I offer you something to eat or drink?'

'Nothing, thank you.' Samira couldn't swallow anything. Her insides felt like they'd been invaded by circling, swooping vultures.

The man excused himself and Samira darted a look at her watch. She was dead on time. It felt like a lifetime had passed since she'd stepped out of her suite downstairs.

Slowly she breathed out, trying to calm her rioting

nerves, but nothing could douse the realisation her whole future rested on this interview.

If she failed... No, she refused to imagine failure. She had to be positive and persuasive. This might be unconventional but Samira would *make* him see how sensible her idea was.

She swallowed hard, squashing the doubts that kept surfacing, and walked towards the windows. Automatically she stretched out a hand to the luxurious silk of the sofa as she passed. It was cool and soft, the lush fabric reassuringly familiar. If she closed her eyes perhaps she could imagine herself in the quiet sanctuary of her work room, surrounded by delicate silks, satins and crêpe de Chine; by damask, velvet and lace.

'Samira.'

She started and turned, her heart thumping out of kilter as her eyes snapped open. There he was, his powerful frame filling the doorway.

Her breath snared, just as it had time and again that last year. She'd been on the brink of womanhood and suddenly noticed her brother's best friend as a *man*. A man who'd evoked disturbing new responses in her awakening body...

Samira dragged in a calming breath, squashing shock at the way awareness prickled the tender flesh of her breasts and belly. She wasn't the untried girl she'd once been.

'Tariq.'

How could she have forgotten those eyes, their remarkable colour legacy of marauding ancestors who'd intermarried along the way? Under slashing dark brows those eyes gleamed with the pure, rich green of deep water and were just as unfathomable.

His expression made her hesitate.

Was she welcome or did the hard set of his jaw indicate displeasure? Was he annoyed she'd used their connection to inveigle a meeting at short notice? No doubt he had huge demands on his time but he could hardly reject her request, given the close links between their kingdoms.

Samira's brow puckered. The Tariq she recalled had been infallibly patient and friendly, even though she'd probably been a nuisance, tagging along behind him and Asim.

'How are you, Samira?' He stepped into the room and the air evaporated from her lungs. He seemed to fill the space even though he stood metres away, watching her with that penetrating stare as if he saw behind the practised façade to the nervous woman beneath.

'Excellent, thank you.' This time when he gestured for her to take a seat she accepted, grateful to relieve her suddenly shaky legs.

She'd known this would be challenging but Tariq was more unsettling than she'd imagined. Not simply because he had the power to grant or deny what she'd set her heart on. But because that useless, feminine part of her she'd thought long-dormant reacted to him in ways she didn't like to contemplate.

As if the lessons of four years ago had been completely forgotten. More, as if the years had peeled back further and she was seventeen again, sexually aware for the first time and fantasising over Tariq. Heat washed her.

'And you? Are you well? You seemed in fine form last night. The crowd responded so well to your speech.' She snapped her teeth shut before she could babble any more. The last thing she needed was for him to think her a brainless chatterbox.

'I am. The evening was a resounding success. Did you enjoy yourself?'

He strolled across the room, making her aware of the flex and bunch of taut muscle under the superb suit as he sat down opposite her, stretching out long, powerful legs that ate into the space between them. She wanted to tuck her feet back under her seat but kept them where they were, determined not to show nerves.

She fixed on her most charming smile, the one that worked no matter how stressed she felt. 'It was a bit of a crush but worth it for the end result.' Her donation—two gowns to be designed exclusively for the highest bidder—had garnered far more than even Celeste had dared hope.

'Are you staying long in Paris?' It was a simple question, a polite conversation starter, yet the keenness of Tariq's scrutiny invested it with extra significance.

Samira shivered. He could have no idea of her mission here. Suddenly panic hit at the thought of how he'd react when he found out. It would be easy enough to turn this instead into a brief, social catch-up. She could walk out the door with her head high and her secret safe.

But the black void of desolation would be waiting to consume her again. Surely she had the gumption to fight for what she craved, rather than admit defeat so easily?

She was the daughter of generations of warriors. It was time she remembered that.

'I'm not sure how long I'll stay.' She smoothed a damp hand over her fitted skirt, telling herself he couldn't see how her fingers trembled. 'It depends.'

He didn't ask the obvious question, giving her an opening, however tenuous, for her proposition. Nervously she shifted in her seat, then realised what she was doing and stilled.

'I was very sorry to hear about your wife.' She'd added her condolences to Asim's note when Tariq's wife had died giving birth to their twins, but this was the first time Samira had seen Tariq since it had happened.

It was the first time she'd seen him in twelve years. Since the winter she'd turned seventeen and his sudden departure had devastated her. He'd even missed Asim's wedding three years ago due to emergency surgery on his appendix.

Now he looked like a stranger, despite those familiar features.

He nodded, his eyes never leaving hers. 'Thank you.'

Silence fell.

'I saw your boys yesterday in the hotel.' It wasn't what she'd meant to say but her carefully rehearsed words disintegrated under his silent regard. 'They look like a happy pair.'

He nodded. 'They are.'

'And full of energy.'

Samira bit her lip. She was babbling again. She had to get a grip.

'They're never still, except when they sleep.' A hint of a smile lurked at the corner of Tariq's mouth and suddenly he wasn't a stern stranger but the friend she remembered from years ago.

Friends she could deal with. It was the potently masculine Tariq who unsettled her. The man whose deep laugh and imposing body awoke longings that had no place in her life.

'They must keep you very busy.' This time her smile was genuine.

'I wouldn't have it any other way.'

Samira nodded. The Tariq she knew would find time for the demands of his small sons, just as he'd found time for his best friend's kid sister. He took duty seriously but, more than that, he was kind. He was the sort of man you could *trust*.

That was why she couldn't shake the outrageous idea that had taken root as she'd watched him last night at the gala. The idea that he held the key to her future happiness.

Samira swallowed hard. She'd known only one trustworthy man, her brother, Asim. The other men in her life,

even her father, had let her down terribly. Could she trust
Tariq not to do that too?

'Samira.'

'Yes?' She looked up to see him lounging back in his
chair, the picture of ease. Yet his eyes were intent.

'What's wrong?'

'Nothing's wrong.' Her laugh sounded woefully uncon-
vincing and caught her up short. She was stronger than
this. Here was her chance to reach out for the one thing
she really wanted in life. Surely she wasn't coward enough
to give up without trying?

'On the contrary.' She sat forward, projecting an air of
certainty she'd mastered in her professional dealings. She
could do this. 'I wanted to see you because I have a proposal to put to you.'

'Really?' Interest sparked in his eyes.

'A rather unusual proposal, but a sound one. I'm sure
you'll see the benefits.'

'I'm sure I will.' He paused. 'When you tell me what
it is.' Those slashing dark eyebrows angled up in query.

Samira leaned closer, suddenly urgent to get this done.
She licked her dry lips, holding his keen gaze.

'I want to marry you.'

CHAPTER TWO

'MARRY YOU?' ANGER splintered through Tariq that Samira should make him the butt of some jest. He sat bolt upright, hands curling tight around the arms of his chair. 'What game is this?'

Marriage was an institution to be taken seriously, as he knew first-hand. Sharp talons dragged deep through his chest; claws clutched at what passed for his heart.

No, marriage wasn't something to joke about, even between old family friends.

Though Samira was more than an old friend, wasn't she?

At one point he'd wanted much more from her. Long-buried sensations bombarded him—lust, regret, weakness. Above all, guilt. For despite the years apart, even throughout his marriage, Tariq had never completely managed to forget her. His one consolation was that no one, least of all Samira, had known. It had been his secret shame.

'It's no game.' Her voice, uneven before, rang clear and proud. Her gaze, which previously had skittered around the room, meshed with his and Tariq breathed hard as fire heated his veins. Those soft sherry eyes had always been amazing. Now, fixed on him so earnestly, they might have melted a lesser man.

But Tariq's strength had been forged and tested well. He wouldn't be bowled over by a beauty's wide eyes. Even if the beauty was Samira, the most stunning woman he'd ever known, the woman he'd once craved body and soul.

'What is it, then?' he barked. 'If not a joke?' His initial instinct—to avoid this meeting—had been right.

'It's a proposal of marriage.' Her voice was crisp and even, as if she had no notion how bizarre her words were.

Slowly Tariq shook his head. He couldn't be hearing this. Asim's little sister proposing marriage! Didn't she know it was a man's place to choose a wife? A woman's to accept?

What sort of tame lapdog did she take him for? The years since they'd known each other yawned into a fathomless gulf. She didn't know him at all.

He shot to his feet and stalked across the room, staring blankly at the city beyond the sound-proofed glass. 'Whatever the game, I don't appreciate it, Samira.' He swung round. 'Does your brother know about this?'

'It has nothing to do with Asim.' She folded her hands in her lap, for all the world as if they were politely discussing the weather. As if she hadn't offered herself to him in marriage.

An image of her last night, svelte and flagrantly feminine in that dark-red dress, filled his head and his temperature soared, his body tightening in all the wrong places. His hands curled into fists as he fought to focus on her words, not her sensual allure. Anger bit deep that, even now, just one look could ignite the fire in his belly.

'What is this about?' Savagely he reined in his temper, drawing on years of practice at patient diplomacy.

'I want to marry you.'

Those brilliant eyes looked up at him and again shock punched him hard in the gut. She looked, and sounded, serious.

For one disquieting moment he felt a quickening in his body, the sharp clench of arousal in his groin, a welling of possessiveness as he took in the pale honey perfection of her features, the sheen of her lush, dark hair and the Cupid's bow of the sexiest mouth he'd ever known.

When she'd been seventeen that mouth, those eyes, the promise of incandescent beauty to come, had sent him back to his homeland, shocked and ashamed by the hot, hungry thoughts that stirred whenever he'd looked at Asim's little sister.

He'd known then that she'd be breath-stopping, just like her mother, who'd been one of the world's great beauties. But the sight of Samira in the flesh, after twelve years of seeing only photos, took his breath away.

He stiffened, forcibly rejecting his body's response.

She sat there with her ankles primly crossed, her hands folded in her lap, saying she wanted to marry him! It was enough to drive a man crazy.

Tariq cupped the back of his neck, tilting his head and rubbing his skin to ease the tightness there.

'I have no idea what foolishness prompted this, Samira.' He paused, telling himself it was impossible that he tasted pleasure at her name on his tongue. 'But you of all people know royal marriages are carefully arranged. You can't just come in here and—'

'Why not?' She cut across his words and it struck Tariq that no one, not even Jasmin when she'd been alive, interrupted him. As Sheikh, his word was law, his status respected. Except, it seemed, by the Princess of Jazeer.

She stood and his eyes lingered on her delectable body in that figure-hugging suit. 'Why can't I arrange my own marriage? My brother didn't wait for advisors to find him a wife. He found Jacqui by himself.'

'That was different.' Tariq gestured with one slashing hand. 'That was a love match. They're crazy for each other.'

Seeing his friend in the throes of love made Tariq uncomfortable. He'd thought Asim was like himself, too focused on the wellbeing of his nation to choose a partner because of emotion.

Tariq's lips flattened. He didn't do emotion. Not that sort. And especially not now. He had no interest in marrying for love.

The idea ate like acid in his belly.

'If you want to get married, ask your brother to find you a suitable husband. He'll do anything to make you happy.'

Tariq was one of the few who understood Asim's fierce protectiveness of his sister. Their childhood, at the mercy of their parents' volatile on-again, off-again relationship, had left them both reluctant to trust anyone.

Was that why Samira was still single at twenty-nine? Traditionally, Jazeeri princesses married much younger, but he suspected his friend Asim had been in no hurry to rush his sister into matrimony after those early experiences of a dysfunctional family.

'I don't want Asim to arrange a suitable match.' She jutted her chin. In a woman less gorgeous, he'd call her expression mulish. 'I know what I want. I want you.'

Again that sudden blast of blistering arousal low in his body. For an instant he was tempted to forget his duty, his dead wife and his self-control, and haul Samira close, teach her the danger of trifling with him.

Only for an instant.

Tariq reminded himself she wasn't talking about sex. If she had been she'd have used a different approach— soft blandishments and seductive caresses. And she'd have worn something slinky and provocative. His nostrils flared as he sucked in air to tight lungs, imagining that soft mouth on him. Arousal weighted his lower body.

'And you're used to getting what you want?'

Abruptly she laughed, shaking her head, and his pulse faltered at the radiance of her smile. 'Only sometimes.'

'Yet you think you can have me for the asking?' Indignation at her presumption clashed with raw, disconcerting lust at the thought of them together and shame at how easily she got under his skin.

She sobered. 'I thought it couldn't hurt to ask.' She hesitated. 'I know this is unconventional. But we're old friends. I thought you'd at least hear me out.'

That was how she saw him? As an old friend? Why Tariq bridled at the idea, he refused to consider.

'Very well. I'll hear you out.' He folded his arms across his chest and waited.

Samira looked at the imposing man before her. He wasn't in a receptive mood. His crossed arms were all bunched muscles. The tendons in his neck were taut and his mouth a flat line. Even his eyes glittered a warning.

Yet still Tariq was the most breathtaking man she'd ever seen. Her stomach turned to treacle as the afternoon sun caught the solid plane of his jaw and the proud thrust of that impressive nose. She wondered how it would feel if, instead of shutting her out, he opened his arms and hauled her close into that broad chest. If he kissed her...

She blinked, suddenly light-headed.

That was *not* what she wanted. Sex had made a fool of her once. She refused to let that happen again. This, what she proposed now, was far more sensible.

Planting her feet more solidly, wishing she weren't quite so dwarfed by him, Samira cleared her throat, mentally flicking through the arguments she'd prepared.

'It's an excellent match,' she began, gathering herself. 'Our countries already have so much in common. I understand your customs and history. I'm not a complete outsider. And by marrying me you'd strengthen your ties with Jazeer.'

'Our ties with Jazeer are already strong.'

Refusing to be deflated, she kept her chin up. 'My background speaks for itself. I was born and bred to royal rank and responsibility. I understand what's expected of a queen and I've got a lifetime's experience of public functions and diplomacy. I understand royal duty and I won't shirk it.'

Expectantly she looked at him. Finally he nodded. 'All useful attributes.' He paused. 'But others could say the same. Your own sister-in-law has adapted well to her new role, and she wasn't born royal.'

Samira exhaled slowly. Had she really expected Tariq to agree instantly? She told herself his wariness was to be expected. He'd adored his first wife and his choice of second wife would affect not only himself but his precious boys and his country. Of course he needed to consider this from all angles.

Yet a small part of her wailed in disappointment that he viewed her so sternly, almost disapprovingly, when her own wayward impulse urged her to close the gap between them. Her very skin felt sensitised, as if longing for his touch.

Did she want him to look at her and *want* her? Not for her pedigree or her social attributes but for *herself*? Her wayward body betrayed her. Her flesh tingled as his gaze raked her and a slow, telling spiral of heat eddied low in her belly.

Samira sucked in a stunned breath, sensing danger.

She told herself it was nerves. The shock of seeing him again after all this time. The disconcerting discovery of how very…male he was.

Once the novelty wore off he'd be just as he'd always been—a friend, someone she could trust. Without trust she couldn't bind herself to any man. Trust had been so lacking in her life, she understood how rare and valuable it was.

The thought gave her renewed energy.

'I'll make a good queen,' she said firmly, locking her

hands together. 'Building my business has given me a chance to step beyond royal boundaries and mix with a range of people, not just wealthy clients. It's broadened my understanding of the world and improved my people skills.' Now she was as at home buying a bagel on the streets of New York as she'd been at last night's A-list gala.

Tariq didn't say anything so she kept talking, the thread of tension wrapping tighter around her insides. 'I'd like to continue working on a small scale, not enough to interfere with any royal duties.' When he remained silent she angled her head higher. 'I believe it would be a positive thing for people to see their queen with responsibilities and successes of her own.'

'You see yourself as a role model, then?'

Samira flinched at the steely glint in his eyes and the sharp pang of shame in her belly. Tariq knew as well as she that her past was tainted by that one, awful mistake she'd made. A mistake that would haunt her all her life.

'No one is perfect, Tariq. Young women in your country could do worse than a queen who's human enough to have made mistakes, yet has learned from them and built something positive for herself.'

Slowly he nodded and a feather of hope brushed her skin, making her shiver with excitement. She leaned closer.

'I'll be a loyal wife and a devoted mother, Tariq. You needn't worry that I'll embarrass you by falling for another man after we're married.' Bile swirled in her stomach and she tasted its bitterness on her tongue. 'I'm not my mother, for ever pining for romantic love. I learned from her mistakes, and my own.'

'You don't want love?' His words were sharp, his gaze intense as he leaned forward. His raised eyebrows signalled surprise, perhaps disapproval. She guessed he was used to women falling at his feet.

Samira's lips twisted. 'Would I be here if I did? If my

mother's example weren't enough, my experience with Jackson Brent cured me of any romantic ideas.'

Jackson Brent. The name no one spoke around her. The man who'd taken her dreams and her innocence and had smashed them in the cruellest way.

She read understanding in Tariq's expression. The whole world knew the story. Samira looked away, pressing her palms to her churning stomach.

Jackson Brent, the sexy film star, had taken one look at Samira, the ridiculously inexperienced princess living away from home for the first time, and decided to have her. Samira, swept off her feet and dazzled by what she thought was love, had believed it a fairy-tale romance come true.

They'd been feted and adored by the press and the public. Until the day Jackson had been found in bed with his beautiful co-star by her vengeful husband.

Samira's cosy world had blown apart, her dreams shattered as she'd been forced to see Jackson as he really was. Not Mr Right, but a feckless, selfish opportunist who'd played on her longing for love to get himself cheap sex and great publicity.

Guessing at her anguish, the press had hounded Samira to the verge of a breakdown—intruding on her privacy, rummaging through her trash, interviewing her friends and turning her heartbreak into fodder for the masses. Till her brother and the woman who'd later become her sister-in-law had helped her get back on her feet, stronger and determined to put the past behind her.

Was it any wonder, after the misery of a childhood watching her parents' marriage teeter from one crisis to another, that she'd finally come to her senses and seen she wasn't cut out for romance? Like her mother, she couldn't trust herself to make the right choice when her heart was involved.

'Samira?'

She turned back, her hands falling to her sides as she registered the concern on Tariq's features.

Instantly she shored up her resolve, locking her knees and straightening her shoulders. She was no longer a victim. She'd dragged herself out of the dark hole of loss and grief that had almost destroyed her.

Tariq didn't need to know those details. About the baby she'd lost before it had even been born. About the grief she carried in her very pores and always would.

Samira blinked and forced herself to concentrate.

'If you're worried about me doing anything scandalous to harm you or your family, don't. My one brush with notoriety was enough.' She might have been the innocent party in the Hollywood scandal but it didn't feel like it, with the press ravenous for every detail.

'You regret the relationship with Brent? You would change the past if you could?'

Samira caught her breath, her fingers threading tightly together. Tariq's directness pulled her up short. Everyone else tiptoed around that episode in her life.

'Oh, yes. I'd change the past if I could. Though...' she paused, remembering that all-too-short period when she'd carried her precious baby '...I can't regret all of it.'

She set her jaw, reminding herself to move on. 'I wouldn't suggest marriage if you were looking for a first wife. But you already have two sons. You can consider taking on a wife who doesn't quite meet all the traditional requirements.'

'Who isn't a virgin, you mean?'

Samira blinked. She couldn't recall Tariq being quite so blunt. The young man she'd known half a lifetime ago had changed since becoming monarch.

Yet she appreciated his frankness. Honesty was the best policy between them. They didn't need misunderstandings.

'All the world knows I once had a lover.' She swallowed over the tight knot in her throat. 'Just as it knows you have lovers.'

Tariq had never been short of female companionship. Since his wife had died he'd been again dubbed one of the world's most eligible men and, according to the whispers Samira heard, there was no shortage of women on hand to ease his broken heart.

'You're very direct.' His eyebrows bunched and she shrugged, refusing to apologise.

'I thought you'd appreciate my honesty, as I appreciate yours. That's what I'd expect in a marriage.'

'Honesty?'

Samira took a half-step forward, drawn by the intensity of his stare.

'Honesty and respect.' She licked her dry lips before continuing. 'I assumed you'd want something similar. That you wouldn't look for love in a second wife. I thought you'd want someone capable, loyal and committed. Someone who could help raise your sons.' Samira paused. 'Was I wrong? Are you looking for romance?'

'Who said I was looking for anything?' His stare was enigmatic, giving nothing away.

Samira spread her hands. 'You have two children under two and a country to run. Your schedule must be manic. But I know you well enough to understand you'll want the best for your boys.' She looked straight into his eyes and was rewarded with the slightest of nods.

'I'm sure you've hired the best staff available to help with them.' Again that infinitesimal nod. 'But no nanny can replace a caring mother. A mother who's committed to being there for them all their lives.'

She drew in a quick breath, knowing her breathing was too shallow, her heart racing, now they came to the crux of it all: the reason she'd braved this almost-stranger and proposed marriage.

'I've always loved children; you know that, Tariq.' Even in her teens she'd taken every opportunity to be with youngsters, getting into trouble for spending too much time playing with the servants' babies in parts of the palace princesses weren't supposed to know existed. 'I'd make a good mother. You can rely on me.'

Tariq wondered if Samira had any idea how appealing she looked, her dark-honey gaze earnest, her expression serious, her hands clasped in unconscious supplication before her.

Unconscious?

Could any woman so beautiful not be aware of her allure?

Yet Samira wore a conservative suit, not a low-cut dress. Her make-up was barely there, her hair neatly up at the back of her head.

And he knew an overwhelming urge to see her panting and flushed, her rich, dark hair in lush abandon around her shoulders, her body bare and inviting.

Desire hammered him, turning muscle and soft tissue into beaten metal, hard and uncompromising. His lungs bellowed as he hauled in oxygen, fighting for control.

The casual way she'd spoken of his lovers, about her own, tugged at something primitive and deep-seated inside him. Tariq knew if ever he possessed Samira he wouldn't share her with anyone else.

And her wistful expression when she'd spoken of her ex-lover, admitting she didn't regret the relationship, even after he'd betrayed her so brutally... Tariq wanted to twist the guy's neck in his bare hands! Brent hadn't deserved her.

He shoved his hands in his trouser pockets. What was he thinking?

Shame smote him, the knowledge that Samira had always been his weakness, even when his loyalties had lain elsewhere. The last thing he needed was to give in to this ancient folly. Besides, saddling himself with a wife was one complication he didn't need.

Yet she was right. A roster of nannies was no long-term solution for his boys. He wanted the best for them. Jasmin had wanted that too and he'd promised her before she'd died...

He scraped the back of his neck with one hand, feeling the iron tension there. Hell! He'd imagined this was some simple social visit from Samira since they were in Paris for the same event. He hadn't expected her to trawl every one of his 'no go' subjects.

'You've spoken about what I'd get out of marriage. But you haven't mentioned why you're so eager for it. Why do you want this?' Tariq didn't know why he was asking. It wasn't going to happen.

But as he surveyed her delicately flushed cheeks, her sinuous body and the long, taut outline of her thighs beneath that pencil skirt, he realised why he kept the conversation going. Because, once conjured, he couldn't erase the image of Samira, abandoned and sexy, in his bed.

Years ago he'd walked away from the teenage Samira because she'd been far too young and he'd been too honourable to act on his desire. That decision had haunted him. The fantasy perfection of 'if only' had overshadowed too many relationships.

But that Samira was gone. She was an experienced woman now, sensual and provocative in ways that spoke directly to his libido.

For long moments Samira said nothing. Her very stillness conveyed tension, heightening his curiosity. Finally she spoke, her gaze settling on a point near his collarbone.

'I want a family.'

'You have family. Your brother and his wife.' But, even as the words emerged, he realised his mistake.

'My *own* family.' Her words confirmed it.

Tariq frowned. 'But why me? Why us?'

He had no false modesty. Acquiring lovers had never been a difficulty. His wealth and status, not to mention his power, attracted many women. But Samira hadn't seemed interested in his royal position, except to prove she was up to the task of being his queen. And as for her being smitten... He narrowed his eyes, watching her steadfastly staring at his collar. She gave no evidence of it.

Annoyance twisted sharply in his belly. He'd grown used to fending off women, not being ignored by them.

He watched her open her lips and found himself wondering if they were as petal-soft as he imagined. The direction of his thoughts sharpened his voice.

'There must be plenty of eligible men. Why not find one you fancy and start a family together? Why come to me?'

Her mouth tightened and she raised her eyes. For an instant he could swear he read pain in that shimmering, gold-flecked gaze. No, not pain. Anguish. Then she blinked, banishing the illusion.

'I told you, I'm not going to be swept off my feet again. I don't want romance.'

Looking down at Samira's beautiful, earnest face, Tariq suddenly felt ancient, like a greybeard surveying an innocent. Was she really too young to understand that was what women did? They fell in love, even if they then lived to regret it. It was in their nature. The heavy thud of his heart against his ribs tolled out the sum of such regrets. He'd grown intimately acquainted with them.

'But taking on someone who already has children—' The expression on her face stopped him midsentence. 'Samira?'

She looked down at her hands. They were clenched together so hard the knuckles whitened. When she met his eyes again, her own looked desolate.

'I want children. I've always wanted them.' She breathed deep. 'But I can't have any of my own.'

Something lodged in Tariq's chest. Something heavy that impaired his breathing. He couldn't imagine the world without his boys so he had some inkling of how bereft Samira felt.

He wanted to reach out and comfort her, pull her in to him and cuddle her, for there was no mistaking her pain. Despite the years since they'd been close, she was still the girl he'd cared for too much.

But he was older and wiser now. At thirty-seven he'd learned there were times when a woman needed her dignity rather than the comfort of an embrace. When nothing he could do would ease the pain.

Memory stabbed hard, slicing through his ribs, tearing at his conscience. Jasmin…

'You see now why I suggested marriage.'

Her quiet words dragged Tariq from a haze of memory and regret. He forced himself to focus.

'You proposed marriage because you want my boys?' Instantly his protective instincts were aroused.

'Don't sound so fierce, Tariq.' She even managed a tiny smile. The sight of it and the sadness in her eyes squeezed his chest. 'I don't want to take them from you.'

She took a step forward, then another, and a waft of light scent filled his nostrils: warm cinnamon and sugar, innocently sweet yet improbably alluring.

'I want to share them with you, look after them, grow to love them and support them.'

'You want to marry me for my *children*?' His mouth firmed. After a lifetime being chased by women, his pride smarted. Was anything designed to puncture a man's ego as much as that?

Did she have any idea of the insult she offered?

He might be a father but he was a red-blooded male

in his prime. A man, moreover, used to being the hunter, not the prey.

Samira stepped closer again, apparently unaware the movement brought her into his personal space. She was so close he felt the warmth of her body, saw the fine-grained perfection of her skin and the tiny shadows beneath her eyes that make-up didn't quite conceal.

'Not just the children, Tariq. I want a family. Someone to belong to. And I can't think of a man I'd rather trust myself with than you. You're decent and honourable.'

Competing emotions battled in Tariq's gut. Pleasure at her belief in him. Annoyance that she saw him as some sort of comforting protector who conveniently had the kids she wanted. And a shudder of carnal pleasure at the sound of his name on her lips, which inevitably led him to imagine her crying it out in the throes of passion.

But she was wrong. He sifted all she'd said, realising it wasn't really him she wanted, but some emasculated version of himself that existed only in her mind.

She didn't know him, had never really known him.

If she had any idea of the darkness within him, or of the urges he suppressed right now—none of them decent or honourable, all of them primitive and utterly indecent—she'd run a mile.

It was time to stop this.

Tariq looked into her eager, open face. 'You honour me with your offer, Samira. But the answer is no. I won't marry you.'

CHAPTER THREE

SAMIRA HAD STEELED herself for rejection but the reality was harder than she'd imagined.

The force of her disappointment threatened to take her out at the knees. Despite spending a lifetime projecting an image of calm, no matter how traumatic her reality, Samira felt her bottom lip begin to quiver.

She bit it. Hard.

She blinked and locked her knees, grateful her skirt hid her shaky legs.

Another second and she summoned up a semblance of a smile, ignoring the stagnant well of disappointment at the heart of her. She breathed deep, as if her lungs didn't feel brittle and papery, like they were about to tear apart.

'Thank you for hearing me out, Tariq.' There, her voice was even and admirably cool. Not the voice of a woman who felt her last hope of happiness had been snatched away.

It had been an outrageous idea. She'd known it from the start. Foolish of her to pursue it.

'I knew even as I asked that I wouldn't suit. You need a much more appropriate wife than I could ever be.'

She glanced around for her bag, only to realise she still wore it over her shoulder. She unclenched her hands and grabbed the thin leather strap for something to do.

'What do you mean, more *appropriate*?' Tariq's searing gaze pinned her to the spot.

'Let's not go there, Tariq. There's no point.' Samira stretched her smile wider and her taut facial muscles ached at the strain. 'It's time I left. I'll say goodbye and wish you and your family all the best for the future. Thank you again for making time to see me.'

She was turning away, desperate to be alone, when long fingers closed around her upper arm.

Instantly she stilled as shock waves ripped through her body.

It had been four years since any man, apart from her brother, had touched her. And this was different—as if a channel of fiery liquid coursed under her skin.

Samira frowned, trying to remember Jackson Brent's touch ever having inflamed such a reaction. But all she could remember were his charming smile, his easy lies and his insistence on kissing her in front of the paparazzi despite her protests.

'What did you mean, Samira?'

Experimentally she tugged her arm. His hold remained firm.

A glance at his face, now close, confirmed he had no intention of relenting.

She remembered that look of adamantine determination from her early teens. Tariq had been visiting Asim and had somehow found out about her one act of rebellion in an otherwise cloistered, well-behaved life. She'd secretly been slipping out, dune-driving without supervision or a crash helmet. He hadn't lectured her. It was as if he'd understood her need to escape her miserable home life, just for a few hours. He'd simply said he knew she had more sense than to risk her neck that way again and made her promise never to drive without him or Asim. He'd known her promise would bind her.

But she wasn't a teenager trying to cope with her parents' manipulation in their battle for supremacy. Why did he drag this out instead of letting her leave with some dignity intact?

She shrugged. 'No doubt your advisors wouldn't approve of you choosing a wife like me.' She took a step away, only to pull up short when he refused to release her.

'First, I make my own decisions, Samira, not my advisors; and second, I don't know what you're talking about.'

Samira whipped around, her eyebrows arching in disbelief. 'Don't be coy, Tariq. We both know I'm tainted.' When his face remained impassive she leaned closer, hurt turning to anger that he made her spell this out. '"Soiled goods", isn't that the phrase?' Her chin hiked up, but given his enormous height she couldn't look down her nose at him. 'In both our countries there are people who disapprove of me, a woman who's never been married but who had a lover.' She tugged in a swift breath. Her heart hammered and her chest rose and fell as if she'd just finished an hour's aerobic workout in the gym. But that was nothing to the distress curling deep inside.

'I thought that wouldn't matter to you since you'd already been married to a virtuous woman who gave you heirs. I'd assumed you weren't hung up on the old ways. But I see I was wrong.'

She'd told herself again and again she had nothing to be ashamed of, having chosen to be with the man she loved. Perhaps that would have been true if Jackson had proved himself worthy of her love. But he'd betrayed her brutally, proved her a fool, her judgement and her dream of love fatally flawed. Instead of the luxury of dealing with her pain and disillusionment privately, it had all been blasted across the press. Her loss of innocence had provided fodder for the voracious masses eager for the story of her heartbreak. She'd felt defiled.

Was it any wonder she refused to trust herself to romance again? No man could tempt her with talk of love. The very idea chilled her to the marrow.

This time she yanked her arm so hard in Tariq's grip it hurt. But still he didn't release her.

Instead he moved closer, dwarfing her with his height and his massive shoulders. But it was his eyes that held her.

'Don't tell me you believe that!' His brow pleated as he looked down at her.

'Why not?' She glared back. 'You're seen with a new woman at almost every social event but none of them last. So it's not as if you're in a relationship and I'm poaching on anyone's territory. I'm suitable, *more* than suitable, in every other way except for that.'

'Your virginity...' he paused on the word and the hairs on the back of her neck rose at his tone '...isn't an issue for me. That might have been relevant a generation or more ago but things have changed.'

'You think?' Samira's laugh was bitter. She surged forward into his personal space as unpleasant memories crowded. 'Tell that to the men who've offered to set me up as their mistress! Men who wouldn't dream of paying court to me as a possible wife. Men whose views haven't quite galloped ahead into the twenty-first century.' She paused, catching her breath, telling herself anger wouldn't change anything. 'Of course you don't want to rock the boat when there are so many who still think that way.'

Tariq's face turned to stone, but his eyes blazed with a heat that almost scared her.

'Who has insulted you like that?' His fingers dug into her arm.

'Tariq! Let me go. You're hurting.' Fear trickled through her insides at his fierce expression. She couldn't recall him ever looking this way. It was like staring into the face of a warrior intent on blood.

'My apologies.' The words were stilted but in an instant his hand was gone, the savage light in his eyes muted.

Yet Samira was still trapped. His big frame cornered her, blocking access to the door.

'*Who* was it?' He growled, the sound tracking across her skin and burrowing deep inside. 'Tell me.'

'Why? There's no point.' Restlessly her fingers slid along the slim strap of her bag. 'I'm not accepting their offers.' She shivered. Such an arrangement would destroy her.

'Does Asim know?'

Samira's lips twisted. 'You think I'd tell my *brother* about that? You have to be joking.'

She'd had enough trouble getting Asim to promise not to lay a hand on Jackson Brent all those years ago. Vengeance wouldn't help, only inflame the situation. Now here was Tariq, looking like he wanted to take somebody apart limb from limb.

A kernel of heat flared in the cold emptiness of her abdomen. He mightn't want her but he cared enough to be incensed on her behalf.

Samira sighed; his protectiveness was one of the attributes that would make him a wonderful husband and father.

She straightened to her full height, wishing she'd worn higher heels so she didn't feel so dwarfed. It wasn't just his size. He bristled with a furious energy that made her far too aware of the solid muscle and power in that long, strong body of his.

She dragged in oxygen, telling herself she wasn't overawed by this macho male. Wasn't her brother another of the same?

Her deep, sustaining breath drew in something new: sandalwood and spice and hot, male flesh. Her nostrils flared eagerly and she stiffened, stunned as a swirl of re-action eddied within.

Samira stepped back, disturbed at the way her body betrayed her.

'Not so fast.' Tariq paced with her, hemming her against a sofa. 'I want to know—'

'No. You don't.' Finally Samira reasserted herself, pro-jecting the composure she gathered about herself when the going got tough. 'It's none of your business, Tariq. You're not my keeper. In fact you've just passed up the opportunity to be anything to me but an old friend. An acquaintance.'

His mouth flattened and she sensed his keen brain sift-ing her words. He didn't like them but there was nothing he could do.

'So, once more, thank you for your time and goodbye.'

She didn't offer to shake hands. The imprint of his touch still burned her upper arm. Not from pain but, she assured herself, because she wasn't used to being so close to a man. The tremulous little stirrings in her belly—the quickened breathing, the reaction to his skin's aroma—were proof of that. It wasn't anything personal.

'Wait.'

Samira hesitated, then slowly lifted her eyes to his. There it was again, a twinge of something that felt far too much like physical awareness.

'What is it?' The words shot out, crisp with challenge.

'Have you asked anyone else?'

Her eyes widened. 'To marry me?' Did he think she'd lined up a list of candidates to interview by the hour?

What sort of woman did he think she was?

Desperate.

The word surfaced despite her efforts to suppress it. And she was. But not desperate enough to do this more than once. Today's humiliation was enough.

Besides, only Tariq had tempted her to think of marriage. There was no other man she trusted enough.

'Only you,' she said at last, daring him to preen at the compliment.

'And will you ask anyone else?' He leaned closer, looming over her as if to intimidate.

Except Samira was undaunted. She might have laid herself open to rejection but she had her pride. That and her determination never to give up were what kept her going. She didn't need his interference or his sympathy.

Anger spiked.

Deliberately she reached out and tweaked the precise knot in his silk tie, twitching it unnecessarily, then patting it in place, ignoring the heat of bone and solid muscle beneath his shirt.

'It's kind of you to be interested in my plans, Tariq, but what I do is none of your business. It ceased to be when you rejected my proposal.' She favoured him with a gracious smile that masked her desire to see him squirm. 'I'll give your regards to Asim and Jacqui when I see them, shall I?'

His hand clamped over hers as she made to withdraw it. He pressed her palm against the crisp, body-warmed cotton of his shirt so she caught the steady, strong beat of his heart beneath her touch. It felt too intimate.

She should have known not to play provocative games with Tariq. He had so much more experience than her.

'Not just yet.' He paused, his keen gaze roving her features. 'Come back tomorrow for my final answer.'

Samira stared back, hope and disbelief vying for supremacy, anticipation stirring. 'You seriously want time to consider?'

His thumb stroked hers in a long sweep, drawing a tiny, jittering reaction through her.

'You raised some persuasive points.' He murmured in

that dangerously deep voice. 'It would be premature to reject the idea out of hand.'

Did he hope to delay long enough to go behind her
back and contact Asim, hoping her brother would scotch
her plans?

As if it mattered. She wasn't in the market for just any
husband. If Tariq turned her down, that was it.

'You've changed your tune.' Samira narrowed her gaze
and pulled her hand from his before the tingling in her fingers spread up her arm.

He shrugged, the movement emphasising his superior
size and strength, but she refused to be intimidated. 'You
took me by surprise. I need to think about it.'

Slowly, Samira nodded. She'd give him the benefit of
the doubt. What other choice did she have? She smiled,
hope rising tentatively, and watched something flicker and
intensify in that deep gaze.

'I understand. It's not a decision to be taken lightly.'
She hesitated, searching for the right words. 'You needn't
worry, either, that I'd interfere with your...*personal* life.'
A flush warmed her cheeks but she ploughed on. It had
to be said and it might be a clinching argument in her fa-
vour. 'I know you have a lot of lovers and I don't expect...'
Samira paused, searching for words.

'You don't expect me to give them up? Is that it? You
give me carte blanche to play the field?' Tariq's tone was
harsh and for some reason she didn't understand why he
looked angry.

Samira frowned, wondering what she'd said to stir his
temper. Surely she was offering the sort of arrangement
any man would appreciate?

She understood his decency, his honour and strength, but
after so many years apart he was a stranger in many ways.

'I'm not looking for love or sex, Tariq.' Valiantly she
suppressed a shudder at the thought of deluding herself

with either, making herself vulnerable again. 'I don't expect you to pretend you feel for me what you did for your first wife.' She'd had her fill of pretence from a man. All she wanted was honesty. 'And it would be unfair to expect you to be celibate. I understand a man like you has needs.'

'Needs?' Tariq's gaze honed to shards of rough-cut emerald.

'Yes.' Samira swallowed, refusing to be daunted, reminding herself that she was worldly and experienced. 'Sexual needs. But it's companionship I want from you, Tariq. Respect and support. The shared bond of caring for your children. A purpose in life.'

She petered to a stop, feeling she'd revealed too much. 'I want to be a reasonable wife, Tariq.'

A reasonable wife.

The words echoed with a dull clang in the void where Tariq's heart supposedly lodged.

He couldn't believe he was hearing this.

Samira—gorgeous, seductive Samira—was offering herself in marriage and telling him in the same breath she didn't want to consummate the arrangement?

How did women come to have such twisted, unfathomable minds?

He'd never heard anything so preposterous.

Marriage to Samira but no sex.

Presumably no touching at all.

No kissing either.

His gaze lingered on the plump bow of her ripe lower lip and a groan rose in his throat, to be savagely repressed. The whole idea was a recipe for madness. He should squash it now before she got her hopes up.

But it was too late. Those stunning eyes shone brighter and she watched him expectantly.

As if at any moment he'd thank her for denying himself the one thing he really wanted. The one thing he'd wanted since he'd seen her again. If he were truthful, that he'd wanted for far too long. Samira. Samira up against the wall of last night's venue, with her long skirt rucked up around her waist as he pleasured her. Samira in his bed, sharing his shower, or breathless beneath him on the long couch just behind her. He'd pictured her on it since he'd walked into the room and saw her caressing it. She was so tactile, a true sensualist.

Samira any way he could get her.

Breathe. Deeper. Slowly.

How could any woman be so naive? Especially a woman with such natural sensuality? It was there in her walk, her love of texture, the way her eyes lingered with that hint of longing that belied the words emerging from her lips.

How could she think of denying them such pleasure?

Yet she thought she was being reasonable, generous, even.

In his years of marriage to Jasmin he'd never considered straying. His word was his bond and he was traditional enough to believe marriage was about loyalty.

'That's noble of you, Samira.' He paused, scarcely believing the words emerging from his mouth. 'I'll give you my answer tomorrow.'

Twenty-six hours later Tariq halted in the doorway to the twins' playroom in the luxury hotel suite. A crisis in Al Sarath had disrupted his schedule and he'd missed his meeting with Samira. She couldn't possibly have waited this long for him.

He'd told himself it was just as well. Yesterday he'd found himself arranging to meet her again, driven by the need to prevent her propositioning someone else.

The thought of her with another man, offering to marry him, even with that crazy 'no sex' stipulation, gouged a chasm through his belly.

He wasn't her keeper.

He didn't want a wife. The thought of replacing Jasmin with Samira made him break out in a sweat. He might lust after her but how could he sign up to another marriage?

Yet for twenty-six hours he'd imagined little else. Her saner argument for marriage—to provide a loving, stable environment for his boys—made sense. Too much sense.

Tariq had put off for too long the need to find a mother for the twins. A warm, gentle woman who'd nurture them. A caring woman who'd love them as Jasmin would have.

A shiver scudded down his spine and the old blackness fringed his vision.

His boys deserved a mother. Already he realised he had to provide more than he could now with his taxing schedule. His wasn't a job he could set aside when family commitments demanded. His country, his people, relied on him.

Now, standing in the shadow of the half-open door, he confronted the most compelling reason yet for action—their happiness. He'd thought Samira had left hours before, but no, she was there, to the delight of his boys.

At the centre of the room his sons sat astride plush cushions filched from the lounge, enthusiastically jogging up and down to the rhythm of Samira's lilting voice. She had a clear contralto voice that tugged at long-forgotten memories of early childhood.

She sang a made-up song about Adil and Risay riding, one on a camel and one on a horse. Each time the boys heard their names they giggled and jogged faster, urging on their imaginary mounts, till at last the song ended.

With a sigh Samira sank back on the carpet, as if exhausted. Instantly the toddlers scrambled off their cushions and across to her. Adil snuggled up at her side and her arm automatically wrapped around him. Risay, more energetic, climbed onto her legs, ready for another ride. Instead of scolding, she laughed before scooping him close.

The three of them lay there. His boys and Samira.

She wore a dress the colour of amethyst that complemented the warm tone of her skin. The flaring skirt with its silky sheen looked indulgently feminine and expensive but there was a dark smear near the waist and a matching mark on her cheek. She'd kicked off her shoes. Her bare feet and legs looked tantalisingly sexy.

Something somersaulted in Tariq's chest as he took in the three of them, his precious sons and the woman who cared less for her expensive clothes than she did for them.

In the far corner of the room Sofia, the nanny, folded clothes, her back turned. The fact that the boys' fierce protector, who'd been with them since the day they'd lost their mother, was relaxed enough not to watch the newcomer like a hawk, told him everything he needed to know. Samira and the boys had clearly bonded.

All that remained was to decide how he felt about that.

For somehow in the last twenty-six hours, her proposal had turned from outrageous to possible.

Samira sighed and cuddled them close, breathing in the smell of baby powder and little boys.

Even if Tariq refused her, these couple of hours had been wonderful. The boys were a delight.

Her heart felt lighter, not just because she'd spent time with two such adorable toddlers but because she'd contributed, helping out while Sofia had packed, keeping the boys constructively amused.

Celeste would tell her she contributed with her fashion designs and charity donations. But there was something innately satisfying about the simple act of caring for this little family.

She breathed deep, knowing it was time to move. The

boys were ready for bed and the longer she stayed the harder it would be to leave. What had begun as a simple invitation to wait for Tariq and meet his boys in the meantime had turned into something far more complex, at least for her eager heart.

She opened her eyes to find Tariq standing over her. He didn't smile and his look was intent, as if he saw right inside her, to longings and regrets she kept strictly private. She felt caught out, at a disadvantage sprawled on the floor, her unguarded emotions too close to the surface.

Abruptly her heart leapt in her breast. Her pulse fluttered as he bent, his hands briefly brushing her as he scooped up Adil, now fast asleep, then left the room with the nanny following.

The gleam in Tariq's clear green gaze unravelled something within her. Something she didn't want to feel. It made her feel too vulnerable. She was still grappling with that, her breath coming too fast, when he returned, lifting a sleepy Risay and taking him to the bedroom.

Quickly she sat up, twisting up her hair into some semblance of order, frantically scanning the floor for her shoes.

'I'm sorry to keep you waiting so long.' Tariq's low voice came while she was on her hands and knees, peering under a settee.

Abruptly she sat back, feeling flushed and dishevelled, especially when Tariq looked just as debonair as ever. A lot of big men couldn't pull that off, appearing either too lean and lanky or so heavy-set you knew they'd run to fat with age. By contrast Tariq was perfectly proportioned and frighteningly attractive.

Samira's heartbeat skidded into a kick start. It was as well he hadn't agreed to marry her—that was clear from his carefully neutral expression. She didn't like the way her body behaved when he was around.

Samira scrambled to her feet, brushing down her dress,

noticing for the first time sticky patches where the boys had shared their food.

'No doubt you had more *important* business to attend to.' More important than declining her proposal. Her mouth tightened.

Only sheer doggedness had made her wait despite the lengthy delay. She was determined to make him say the words to her face, despite the temptation to avoid further embarrassment and slink away. She tilted her chin. She was a princess of Jazeer. She would see this through.

'You don't understand.'

'There's no need to explain.' He'd already made his position clear. 'I understand perfectly.'

'There's a crisis in Al Sarath. I've been dealing with it long-distance.'

Samira froze. 'A crisis?'

'One of the provinces has been hit by severe flash flooding in the mountain ravines. It's wiped away whole villages.'

Samira sucked in her breath, indignation fading as the import of his words hit. The mountain provinces were the poorest in his country. She remembered adobe houses perched in arid gullies so steep they became death traps on the rare occasions distant mountain rains brought unaccustomed water.

'I'm so sorry.' Guilt pierced at her petty indignation. No wonder he was late! 'You must be wishing you were there.'

He nodded, his expression sombre. 'We fly out soon. I need to be on the ground.'

'Then I won't keep you.' Relief filled her as she spied her shoes beneath a jumble of wooden blocks.

'You don't want to hear my decision?'

His voice stopped her as she bent, reaching for her discarded heels. Slowly she straightened. There was no chance Tariq would change his mind. He'd been dead set against the idea, even outraged. And now… She looked up into a penetrating stare that gave nothing away. He didn't look like a man about to grant her wish.

He was so stern, as if she represented a problem he had to tackle.

Again she wondered if Tariq would go behind her back to her brother, warning him she was going off the rails.

The idea almost made her smile. Asim had worried about her for too long—not because she was wildly kicking over the traces, but because she buried herself in her work instead of 'embracing life'. She knew he secretly feared she hadn't fully recovered from what had happened four years before. Surely propositioning his best friend counted as embracing life?

'Of course I want to hear. That's why I'm here.' But she refused to feel even a scintilla of hope. He'd given her no encouragement, not even a smile.

She almost began to be thankful. It had been a lunatic idea. Imagine her and Tariq…

He closed the space between them with one long stride, making her more aware than ever of their physical differences. Barefoot, she scarcely came up to his shoulder.

One large, warm hand closed around hers, lifting it high. Tariq bent his head, the light catching the blue-black sheen of his thick hair. Samira felt the press of surprisingly soft lips on the back of her hand as he made a courtly gesture that sent a shocking thrill right through her body.

Her breath was a sudden hiss, her lungs pumping like bellows as he lifted his eyes to hers. This time his expression wasn't grim or guarded. It was full of anticipation.

'You honour me greatly with your proposal, Princess Samira.' He smiled and the world tilted around them. 'I accept with pleasure. We'll be married as soon as it can be arranged.'

CHAPTER FOUR

'AT LAST! AFTER five days of celebrating we finally get to the wedding. These royal events are a real test of stamina.'

Samira looked at her sister-in-law, Jacqui, lounging on a couch, taking a glossy cherry from a silver bowl.

'How can you eat?' Samira's stomach was performing a nervous twist and dip that would have done an Olympic diver proud.

She had to call on all her years of training to sit still, rather than shift edgily and risk smearing the intricate henna patterns being painted on her hands and feet. Two ladies-in-waiting sat before her, creating the traditional designs.

Bridal designs.

For the first time, today, the wedding became real.

The official functions so far had been comfortingly familiar, like untold numbers of royal celebrations she'd attended in the past. Why that should be comforting, Samira didn't know. This marriage was her idea. It would be wonderful for all of them: her, Tariq and the boys.

Yet suddenly today she felt ridiculously wobbly.

Bridal nerves were normal, she assured herself. Even if she wasn't a bride in the usual sense.

Most brides looked forward to a night in their new husband's arms.

Her insides cramped and the skin at her nape prickled. Samira's brain seized at the thought of complicating this carefully planned arrangement with sex. Already she felt she walked a knife edge. Her unbidden physical awareness of Tariq was a constant undercurrent. As if there was a disconnect between her mind, that knew intimacy would be a mistake, and her body, that trembled at his touch.

'You think I should stop eating because of the upcoming banquet?' Jacqui shook her tawny head ruefully. 'I never used to have much of an appetite.' Her other hand slipped to the baby bump barely visible beneath her aquamarine top. 'But I've never been so hungry.'

'Except last time you were pregnant.'

'You're right. I was ravenous then too.' Jacqui laughed and Samira smiled. Jacqui distracted her from the anxiety that had somehow grown to a peak of apprehension.

'Pregnancy suits you. You really are glowing.' Samira smiled, feeling only the tiniest flicker of envy. She'd come to terms with her barrenness and couldn't begrudge another woman such happiness. Instead she basked in familiar warmth at the thought of her brother's family. Jacqui was the sister she'd never had, loving and supportive. She almost made Samira wish she could have what Jacqui had: a marriage based on love.

But that wasn't for her. She knew too well she wasn't cut out for that.

There was a bustle as her attendants rose and all four women admired the results. Samira's hands, wrists, feet and ankles were works of art, covered in ancient designs that proclaimed her royal lineage as well as talismans of good fortune, happiness and fertility.

She swallowed, ignoring a pang of regret. There was no sense pining over what could never be. She was the luckiest of women, about to acquire a wonderful husband she could respect and trust and two delightful sons. She could ask for nothing more.

Samira thanked the women warmly. When they'd left, Jacqui put aside the bowl of cherries and sat up.

'Now, do you want to tell me what's wrong?'

'Wrong?' Samira stared. 'Nothing. Tariq has done everything to make the celebrations a huge success. And the ceremony this afternoon—'

'The celebrations. The ceremony.' Jacqui waved her hand dismissively. 'They're spectacular and the whole country is enjoying them.' She leaned closer, her gaze appraising. 'But I look at you and I don't see a bride.'

'You don't?' Samira stared at the wedding patterns staining her skin, then across to the table littered with ornate jewellery. Gold, rubies and huge antique pearls caught the light. On the other side of the room hung her bridal gown, the sumptuous cloth of gold shimmering.

Jacqui followed her gaze. 'The trappings are there, but something is missing.' There was concern in her eyes. 'You don't look like a woman in love.'

Samira flinched, then made herself smile. She was making the best of her life, choosing hope over regret instead of locking herself away to fret over what she'd lost. She would build something positive and make a useful contribution, helping to raise a family.

She was being strong.

And, if the best she could hope to achieve didn't include romantic love, that suited her. She was far better without that.

'Not all brides are in love, Jacqui. Arranged marriages are common, especially between royals.'

'I know, I know. Asim said the same.'

Samira tensed. Jacqui had discussed this with Asim? She hated that she'd been the subject of such discussion, even though she knew it was because they cared for her. They'd been there when she'd needed them in her darkest hours. But she was fine now.

'It's just that I want you to have what I have, Samira.' Jacqui looked so earnest. 'I want you to be happy, to be loved and in love.'

'Thank you.' She reached out and touched Jacqui's arm. 'But I *am* happy. This is exactly what I want.'

Still her sister-in-law frowned.

'Not everyone wants to fall in love. Asim must have told you about our parents.'

Solemnly Jacqui nodded. 'They were unhappy.'

Samira's huff of laughter was bitter. 'They were miserable and they made life hell for us too. They were either so in love no one else mattered, or they were fighting like wild cats, doing anything to score a point over the other, even using us in their battles.' She looked down to find herself pleating the fine fabric of her skirt. Her chest tightened.

'Your parents were volatile and self-indulgent.' Jacqui's voice penetrated the memories. 'Love needn't be like that.'

'I know and I can't tell you how happy I am for you and Asim.' Samira paused. 'But I don't want love. I tried that and it was the biggest mistake of my life. I'm too much like my mother. I was swept off my feet by romantic dreams, blindly putting my trust in someone completely wrong for me.'

'Jackson Brent is a louse,' Jacqui growled. 'You can't blame yourself.'

Samira sat back in her chair, warmth filling her at her sister-in-law's instant support.

'I do blame myself. I wasn't a child. I made the decision to throw everything over, all I'd worked for and dreamed of, to be with him. I fooled myself into believing in him and I was utterly, devastatingly wrong.' Her palm crept across her belly as if to prevent the clenching pain, a phantom memory from four years ago.

'One mistake...'

'That was enough. What if I made the same mistake

again? I can't go through that again, Jacqui, I just can't.'
Samira ducked her head, ashamed at the welling distress
that filled her even after all this time. She drew a calming breath. 'I'm too like my mother. I let passion override
judgement and I paid the price. But unlike her I won't make
the mistake of staying on that merry-go-round.'

'And Tariq knows this?'

'Of course he knows.' Samira smiled, her confidence
returning. 'Don't look so worried. This marriage is everything I want.'

'Samira.' Her name on Tariq's tongue made her blink. It
sounded...different. The noise of the wedding banquet
faded as she met his eyes.

Or was it she who was different? Hours spent at his
side through the wedding ceremony and celebration had
left her unaccountably on edge. She felt his presence with
every cell of her body.

Applause filled the feasting hall as he took her hand
and stood, drawing her up. He was resplendent in robes as
white as the distant snow-capped peaks. His jaw was lean
and hard, a study in power, his eyes a glint of cool green
as he looked down at her and slowly smiled.

Instantly heat shimmered under her skin, a heat that intensified when his warm fingers slid against hers, enfolding them completely. Sensation trickled through her from
her tight lungs, meandering all the way down through her
belly to a single pulse point between her legs.

She inhaled sharply, eyes widening as he held her gaze.
There *was* something different about Tariq. Something
she couldn't identify.

'My queen,' he said in a voice barely above a whisper,
yet it amplified in her ears, blotting out the sound of their
guests. Or perhaps that was the thud of her pulse.

'Your Highness.' She dipped her gaze in acknowledge-ment. She owed him her loyalty as her new sovereign.

His fingers tightened around hers, making her look up.

'Your husband.' His nostrils flared as if drawing in her scent and shock buffeted her. Tariq looked so intent, so *close*, his tall frame blocking out everything else. Samira felt a heavy throb of anticipation deep inside as his head lowered purposefully towards hers.

Instantly, disconcertingly, anxiety shredded her com-posure. It was all she could do not to step back, but she was sure he felt the flinch of her hand in his.

His eyes narrowed, a twitch of a frown marking his brow. Then he lifted her hand. She watched him press a kiss to the delicate, hennaed pattern on her flesh and felt the warmth of those firm lips.

Her breath hitched, her breasts rising hard beneath the ponderous weight of ancient gold jewellery that suddenly seemed far too oppressive.

Tariq smiled. She felt the movement against her hand and wondered, dazed, what amused him. Finally, eyes still meshed with hers, he straightened to his full height.

The crowd stood, applauding so loud it was a wonder the crystal glassware on the tables didn't shatter.

A herald appeared before them, bearing a golden gob-let studded with cabochon emeralds and amethysts. Tariq took it in one large hand.

'Long life to the happy couple,' roared the herald.

Tariq lifted the goblet and drank, then held it out to Samira, turning it so her lips touched the spot from which he'd drunk. Heat sizzled through her as he watched her over the rim and she swallowed the heady, sweet mixture that tasted of honey, cinnamon and unknown spices.

'May they be blessed with peace and happiness and honoured by all.'

Again Tariq drank. Samira watched, enthralled, as the muscles in his powerful neck moved.

He held the drink out to her, again presenting her with the same side of the goblet that he'd used. She told herself she imagined the taste of him there on the beaten gold. Yet it felt incredibly intimate, pressing her lips where his had been, even though she knew it was merely a symbolic gesture as old as the traditional marriage ceremony. She gulped a little too much, feeling the concoction catch the back of her throat.

Tariq's hand squeezed hers and Samira's tension eased a little. It would be all right. They were almost through the celebration that had somehow turned into an ordeal.

'And may they be blessed with strong, fine children.'

Samira was ready for it but still the words caught her a slashing blow to the midriff. She pasted on a bright smile and watched Tariq draw a deep draft from the golden chalice.

He lifted it to her mouth, tilting high so she had no choice but to swallow more than the tiny sip she'd planned.

The hall broke out into a pandemonium of applause and ululating cheers. But all she could see was Tariq's eyes. They'd darkened to gleaming tourmaline. Or were her senses blurring? She felt warm and somehow...undone.

Tariq lowered the goblet and Samira licked her bottom lip, catching a stray drop that lingered there. Tariq seemed fascinated with the movement and to her horror she felt tiny prickling darts of heat pepper her breasts and abdomen. Just as if he'd touched her.

Heat burned in her ears.

'What is that stuff?' she whispered.

He passed the goblet to the waiting herald, his eyes never leaving hers. 'It's harmless enough. A traditional mixture designed to promote virility.'

Samira snapped her mouth shut, her brain whirling as

Tariq turned to address the assembled throng. She told her-self it was a necessary part of the ritual, no more. But the feel of Tariq's hand still gripping hers, the sensation of his long fingers threading through hers, his thumb stroking her palm, sent a warning buzzing through her.

Tariq watched from the doorway as his bride bent over the twin beds where his boys slept. A nightlight glowed at floor level and she looked like something from a fairy story, all shimmer and fragile, gossamer-fine fabrics.

But Samira wasn't an ethereal fairy. She was a warm, flesh-and-blood woman. He'd felt her pulse stir as he held her hand at the banquet, watched the rosy heat brighten her cheeks and plump up her lips as she drank their wed-ding toast.

His groin had tightened unbearably as he'd looked down into those wide, anxious eyes and he'd felt the double-edged sword of lust and caution at his throat. He wanted her so badly his skin grated with it.

It felt like he'd wanted Samira most of his life.

Now there was nothing, not even the guilt he carried over Jasmin, to stop him having her.

Yet seeing her bent over his sleeping sons, rearrang-ing blankets and moving stuffed toys, he felt more than desire. Gratitude that she genuinely cared for them. How many other brides would have spent their wedding night checking on their stepchildren?

Yet wasn't that why she'd proposed marriage? For his children?

Tariq's jaw tightened. His pride shrieked outrage that she saw him as no more than a tool to get what she wanted.

He'd read her expression when she'd told him she couldn't have a baby. He'd seen her pain and it was part of the reason he'd consented to this marriage, despite his reservations. That and the curious certainty he couldn't simply turn his back on Samira as originally intended. She had something he needed.

It had given insight into her motivation for brazenly offering herself in marriage. And he'd been determined she'd make that offer to no other man but him!

Tariq spun away on his heel and stalked down the corridor. But Samira didn't offer herself, did she? She expected him to accept her with conditions. As if he wasn't a man with a man's needs and hungers. As if he didn't have a right to touch the woman who'd pledged herself to him, body and soul.

She'd thought she could dictate terms to him, the Sheikh of Al Sarath!

Perhaps she was more innocent than the world thought. He could have told her no marriage was as simple as it appeared on paper, not when it was lived by real people. Not even an arranged marriage executed for reasons of pragmatism and convenience.

A clammy hand wrapped around his chest, squeezing tight as shadows of the past rose.

When two people lived together as husband and wife the boundaries blurred. And in this marriage, despite Samira's fond imaginings, the boundaries were about to be ripped asunder.

Samira leaned back against the pillows, a paperback in her hand. A gentle breeze stirred the long, sheer curtains and soft lamplight made even the enormous, lavishly appointed room seem cosy. Yet she was too wired to relax.

Her mind buzzed with impressions. The noise and colour of the crowd at the wedding. The strange sense that, despite the throng, she and Tariq were isolated from the rest, each action, each word, weighted and momentous. The spicy smell of Tariq's skin as he'd held her hand and kissed it. The way his eyes had held hers as they'd shared that jewelled goblet.

That must be it, the reason her body was tight and achy. It was the potion they'd drunk. The alternative, that this was a reaction to Tariq, just wasn't acceptable.

Or perhaps it was the suspicion, fuelled by the gleam in Tariq's eyes today, that there might be complications in their marriage-on-paper-only arrangement. That look reminded her Tariq was a virile, red-blooded man used to taking what he wanted.

Samira rubbed at the goose bumps on her arms, telling herself she was being fanciful. Tariq had accepted her terms.

She turned to switch off the lamp and caught movement on the other side of the room.

'Tariq!' Her voice was a thready whisper.

He'd changed out of his wedding finery. Gone was the white robe and head scarf. Gone was the jewelled, ceremonial dagger. Gone was half his clothing!

This was Tariq as she'd never seen him. Her eyes rounded and her jaw sank open. The young man she'd once known had been long and lean but his body had changed in a decade, filling out the promise of those wide shoulders.

Her vision was filled with acres of bare, golden skin. She drank in the solidly muscled pectorals dusted with dark hair, the flex and bunch of more muscles at his taut abdomen as he prowled out of the shadows towards her. He walked proud, shoulders back, stride confident, reminding her that this man ruled all he surveyed.

Samira's throat dried as she took in the splendour of him. He was like a statue of a Greek god come to life—all warm flesh instead of cold marble. A long silver, slashing arc across his ribs and another smaller scar near his shoulder were the only things marring that perfection.

Yet they emphasised his earthy masculinity. She knew

he'd got the larger wound in his teens, practising the ancient art of swordsmanship. She'd heard him tell Asim that his uncle, who was his guardian, had given him no sympathy because he'd been foolish enough not to wear protective clothing, and worse, to let someone get the better of him. Tariq had grown up in a man's world where toughness was prized and no quarter was given for sentiment or weakness. Now he looked every inch the marauding male.

Not like a man committed to a platonic relationship.

A shiver ran through her, tightening her muscles and rippling across her skin. Her breath hissed between her teeth.

Her eyes dropped to the pale, loose trousers he wore, riding dangerously low.

Awareness slammed into her and she struggled back against the headboard, realising too late she was staring.

'What are you doing here?' Her voice was half-strangled in her throat.

'I came to wish my bride goodnight.' His mouth tipped up in a smile that was at once easy and far too disturbing, as it set her already racing pulse skittering out of control. 'It's customary between married couples.'

'But I... But we're not...'

'Not married? I think you'll find we are, Samira.'

His smile widened, grew sharp as his gaze dropped to her lips, then lower to her full breasts straining against the oyster satin nightgown. Instantly her nipples hardened, thrusting against the soft fabric. She crossed her arms, hiding them from view.

'I didn't expect to see you again tonight,' she said, mustering her control. Uneasily she watched him near the bed. He was so tall he loomed over it but she refused to shrink back. She had nothing to fear from Tariq. She'd known him, trusted him, as long as she could recall. Just because her traitorous body yearned for him, she was imagining he felt the same.

'You wanted a husband and family,' he said smoothly, as if he were right at home in her bedroom. She wished she had his sangfroid. She felt as out of her depth as a frightened virgin. 'Your life has changed, Samira. You need to accept that. You won't just see me at formal functions but at all hours, including the middle of the night if the boys are sick or need us. Even with the help of nannies you'll be on tap, not just when they're already bathed, fed and dressed.'

'Of course. I know that.' She nodded, breathing more easily. The reminder of the boys grounded her, easing her nerves at Tariq's presence. She leaned forward, relieved to be on solid ground. 'I went along to see them. They were sleeping soundly.'

'But you kissed them goodnight anyway.'

'How did you know?' Did he object? Did he think she was trying to take Jasmin's place? She was conscious that she'd stepped into the slippers of a dead woman.

'I saw you.'

Her head swung higher.

'You did? I didn't see you.'

He shrugged. 'I thought I'd give you time alone with them.'

Samira's lips curved in a smile. This was the Tariq she remembered: kind and thoughtful. Caring.

'Thank you,' she murmured. 'But you should have come in. I wouldn't want to keep you away from them.'

'I'm here now.' Suddenly he was sitting on the side of the bed, turned to face her, his hand planted beside her silk-clad hip, hemming her in. Shock ricocheted through her.

Furtively she moistened her bottom lip with her tongue. Whenever Tariq got this close her mouth parched.

'Is there anything you want?' Samira fought nervous tension and smiled at him. There were hundreds of reasons for him to stop by for a midnight chat. Arrangements to farewell the VIP guests tomorrow, her family included. Or perhaps some detail about the boys' routine.

'Yes.' The word was a low hum that stirred the butterflies nesting in her belly. 'A goodnight kiss.'

'A—?' She goggled. She couldn't be hearing right. Samira shook her head, loose tresses sliding around her bare shoulders.

'Kiss.' He said it again, his face serious. His gaze dropped to her mouth and heat roared through her. Samira swallowed, her arms wrapping tighter across her torso. Her breasts felt too full and highly sensitised, the nipples blatantly puckering.

'But...why?'

She halted, her face flaming as realisation hit. She'd never felt so gauche. She wasn't some innocent. She understood what it meant when a half-naked man entered his wife's bedroom at night and demanded a kiss. 'That's not what we agreed,' she said quickly. 'It's not part of our deal.'

'Your deal, Samira. Not mine.'

Her fingers gripped her upper arms like claws, digging into soft flesh. This couldn't be happening. 'But you heard me out. You understood.'

'I heard you explain you wanted a marriage that was no marriage.' He leaned infinitesimally closer and the air between them clogged. She couldn't seem to draw enough oxygen into her lungs. 'That doesn't mean I agreed. What I agreed was to make you my wife. That's exactly what I intend to do.'

Shock battered her as she read his intent. And a sense of betrayal so deep it sliced straight to her heart.

She'd *trusted* Tariq. That was why she'd approached him of all men. She knew his word was his bond and he'd implicitly accepted the conditions she'd put on their marriage. Yet now...

Bile rose in her throat. She could barely believe she'd been duped again by a man, and by *this* man.

He hadn't told her his intentions before the wedding. He'd waited till it was too late for her to withdraw.

He'd tricked her.

'Tariq!' Her voice was a hoarse scratch. 'As a man of honour—'

His finger on her lips silenced her. She gasped and tasted the salty, male tang of him. To her dismay she registered how good that tasted.

Samira became conscious of the way he caged her against the headboard. His other arm reached across her, his hand planted on the bed beside her hip, trapping her.

'No man of honour would accept what you proposed, Samira. Not if he had any self-respect.' He watched her closely, as if cataloguing her reaction. 'You came to the wrong man if you wanted some emasculated father figure.'

'Father figure?' Her eyes rounded. 'The last thing I want is to tie myself to a man like my father.' He'd been emotionally unstable, lacking in judgement and self-control. It was his example, and Brent's, that had driven her to seek marriage with someone dependable.

Tariq didn't look dependable right now. He looked unpredictable and dangerous, like a keen-eyed hunter sighting his prey.

Fear trickled down her spine.

'You're too young to be a father figure to me, Tariq.'

He shrugged and her mouth dried a little more. She stood no chance against his strength if he decided...

'You wouldn't force me!' The words shot out defiantly, yet she couldn't quite disguise the question in them.

Tariq reared back, his eyes flashing as if she'd insulted his manhood. 'Of course not. I'd never force a woman!' He lifted his hand from the bed as if to break that sense of entrapment. But it was too late. Samira was transfixed.

'Tell me what you want, then.' She swallowed hard but jutted her chin defiantly. She wouldn't give in without a fight.

'Just a kiss.' His eyes held hers. 'When I went to kiss you at the banquet in front of our guests, you turned as pale as milk.' He nodded as her mouth flattened. It was true. She hadn't been able to hide her reaction.

Relief flooded her, weakening her limbs. A kiss, that was all, not…

Her brain seized at the alternative.

'I refuse to have a wife who's afraid of me. Who can't bear to be close to me.' Something dark flashed in his narrowed eyes and her heart pounded faster. 'I need a wife who can take her place at my side without flinching.'

'I'm sorry,' she murmured stiffly. 'I don't know what happened.' Except she did. She'd seen Tariq the man, not the convenient spouse, and been terrified by her response. 'But we don't have to kiss.'

'Can you think of a better way to prove you won't cringe away next time I'm near you? The next time we're together in public? And there are the boys to consider. I don't want them thinking I intimidate you.' His deep voice held a hollow note she hadn't heard before.

Suddenly Samira saw herself as she must seem to him. Needy. Damaged. All the things she'd promised herself she'd never be again. Shame filled her.

She'd promised Tariq she'd be his partner, not an albatross around his neck. Despite his attempt to change the rules of their marriage, pride dictated she give him this much.

'That's all?' Her voice sounded scratchy and breathless. She couldn't dismiss his statement that he hadn't agreed to her marriage terms. But this wasn't the time or place to deal with that. She'd do it when they were fully clothed.

'That's all.'

'And then you'll leave?'

He nodded.

If she kissed him!

Her heart raced out of control at the thought.

Before Samira could have second thoughts she unwrapped her arms and braced her hands on the bed either side of her. A quick breath dragged in the disturbingly appealing scent of Tariq's warm skin, but she refused to think about it, or the way his eyes darkened as she closed the gap between them.

But there was no mistaking the imposing, masculine bulk of him, the bare-chested arrogance of him, or the skirling twist deep inside as she drew close. It made her lose her nerve.

At the last moment she turned her head, pressing her lips not to his mouth but to the firm, taut skin of his cheek. It was smooth, as if he'd just shaved, and it was surprisingly enticing. For an instant she hovered there, her mouth to his flesh, knowing an unheralded desire to explore, to lift her palms to his shoulders and angle her mouth over his.

With a gasp she pulled back, sliding her hands beneath her legs as if to stop them reaching for him again. Her sudden neediness scared her.

Eyes brilliant as gems held hers as blood pounded in her ears. He didn't say anything, though it was obvious she hadn't delivered a real kiss. It was a coward's kiss.

But it was the best Samira could do. Being close to Tariq made her pulse crazy and tied her in knots. Anxiety still feathered her backbone. Did he really intend to demand more?

Abruptly Tariq stood. Samira blinked, her gaze sliding over his amazing bronzed body.

Surely it wasn't regret she felt because he was leaving?

Recognising that she didn't want him to leave stole her voice.

'That's a start,' he murmured finally.

'A start?'

Tariq nodded. 'One day soon we'll be husband and wife in every sense of the word.'

Samira shook her head. He had it all wrong.

'Not because I demand it but because it's what we both want.' He leaned close, his eyes tourmaline shards that dared her to deny it. 'I promise you, Samira, you'll be with me every step of the way.' It was a threat but it sounded like a promise. A promise that sounded appallingly enticing.

She wanted to object, argue, say something to puncture his arrogant certainty. But instead her tongue cleaved to the roof of her mouth.

His gaze scorched and Samira felt the sizzle in every inch of her body. His slow smile hitched his mouth up at one side, creating a sexy groove down one cheek that made her insides clutch. He looked so utterly confident, as if he'd never had a doubt in his life.

'The next time you kiss me it won't be because I ask, Samira, but because you want me.'

CHAPTER FIVE

She was at his side as they said farewell to their guests. Her dress, the colour of sun-ripened peaches, made her glow and brought out the brightness of her warm, sherry eyes. He'd guess that no one else noticed the smudges under her eyes. If they did they'd assume it was because he'd kept her from sleep with a night of unbridled passion. Even her blush looked like that of a new bride.

Tariq's belly clenched. Just thinking about Samira strung him tight as a bow. It was unnatural for a man and wife to live as celibate strangers, even for a night.

But Samira hadn't been ready. She'd been as uptight as a virgin, her nervousness palpable despite her bravado.

He wasn't a man to force any woman. That flash of fear in her eyes had stopped him in his tracks.

Yet he intended to have her as his wife in every sense. He only hoped he survived to enjoy her surrender. His hunger for her was stronger, richer, more compelling than it had been all those years ago. He ached with it.

Because she was the woman he'd desired and never had?

Because she'd been the object of his first real passion?

Stretching out his hand, he placed his palm on her back as she wished a visiting princess a safe trip. Samira stiffened but didn't move away. After a few moments, when his hand didn't shift, he felt her tension gradually ease.

Tariq suppressed a smile as he listened to a guest enthuse about yesterday's wedding celebration. It was like breaking in a filly, getting Samira used to his touch, persuading her to trust him. It would take patience but the prize would be worth it.

He glanced down, taking in her vibrant loveliness. Not just her exquisite features, but the warmth of her personality. Her hand fluttered as she emphasised a point and the delicate henna markings caught his eye. Markings that proclaimed her *his*.

Tariq stiffened as need cannoned into him.

He'd married Samira for all the sensible reasons she'd put forward, including his need to do the best for his boys. He'd responded to the desperation he'd read in Samira, the bone-deep instinct that told him she needed this, needed *him*, more than she was prepared to admit.

But there was one reason above all why he'd accepted her proposal.

He'd never wanted a woman as badly as he wanted Samira.

The truth buffeted him, dragging the air from his lungs. It was a truth he'd tried so hard to ignore.

At seventeen she'd been heartbreakingly lovely. Enough to send him rushing back to his homeland lest he do something unforgivable, like seduce his best friend's innocent sister. He'd felt guilty for years, knowing how dishonourable the carnal thoughts were that plagued him. He'd even, at one point, contemplated offering marriage, till he'd heard she had her sights set on a career in fashion. Tariq had needed a wife by his side, not living in the USA or Europe.

Yet, even in the years they'd been apart, just the sight of her photo in the press had the capacity to distract him. He'd never been able to forget her.

So when she'd come to him for help, offering herself in marriage…

He might be Sheikh, commander, ruler and protector of his people. But he was a man too.

'I wish you well, Tariq,' the visiting prince before him said. 'May your sons be many and strong, your daughters as beautiful as your lovely bride and your years long.'

Tariq clasped his outstretched hand, responding in kind.

It struck him how hard this must be for Samira, with everyone wishing them the blessing of children when she couldn't have any. Regret lanced him and he felt a sliver of hurt for her sake.

Yet she didn't flinch as one after another departing guest offered the same wishes. She was the ideal hostess, regal yet warm, charming and lovely, as if she hadn't a care in the world.

Tariq slid his hand in a comforting circle just above her waist. Would she realise he silently offered his support? He could do no more, not in public and not, he guessed, with a woman who guarded her emotions so closely.

Tariq's gentle caress at her back was strangely soothing. After last night she'd been on tenterhooks, anticipating the next time he'd reach for her, maybe demand another kiss. But this—she shifted her weight rather than press back against his warm hand—this felt like comfort.

At last the guests were gone and they were alone. Still his hand remained, his long fingers splaying heat across her upper back. She should move away.

'How are you holding up, Samira?'

She looked up and was surprised to read concern in Tariq's eyes.

'Okay, thanks.' Her brows twitched together. 'Why, don't I look it?' She'd done her best to disguise her sleepless night.

He shrugged and she felt the shift of his arm across her back. She'd forgotten how good it felt to be touched.

'You look gorgeous.' The gleam in his eyes did strange things to her insides. 'But with everyone harping on the prospect of children I wondered.'

Samira stiffened and stepped away, drawing in on herself. Instantly she missed his touch. She was torn between gratitude that he'd thought of her pain and fear she'd given herself away when she'd prided herself on being strong.

'It's nothing.' His steady scrutiny made her edgy. 'At least, I'm used to it.' She forced a smile to hide her discomfort. So many good wishes for something that could never be had reawakened that dull ache of pain at her core. She refused to give in to it. 'After the first hundred times, it's water off a duck's back.'

'It's over now,' he murmured, as if they didn't both know that for a lie. The speculation would start in a few months when people began looking for signs of pregnancy.

Samira's empty womb contracted hard but she ignored it. She couldn't have her own babies but she was now the mother of two sons. That would keep her too busy to worry about anything else. That and dealing with her new husband.

'As you say.' She nodded. 'It's all over.' His kind lie reassured her that she hadn't quite made the huge mistake she'd feared. Relief welled.

Last night Tariq had shattered her optimism with his declaration that he intended them to be lovers. She'd felt devastated and betrayed, haunted by the fear she'd once again chosen a man she couldn't trust. But now, reading the protectiveness in his body language and the concern in his eyes, she saw the man she'd once known and adored. The decent, caring man she'd thought she'd married.

'Finally we're alone,' he murmured. Samira stiffened, anxiety punching hard and low as he reached for her. His fingers wove through hers, big and strong, effective as any manacle as he turned towards the private royal entrance to the audience chamber. 'Come.'

'Where are we going?' Her breath hitched, distrust rising anew. It struck her that she no longer knew what to expect from the man she'd married.

He paused and looked down. She felt as if she was drowning in those clear, green depths. Had they always been so mesmerising?

'It's our honeymoon. We've got a week with not one official function. There are better places to spend it than the audience chamber.' His mouth tilted in a slow smile that sent fear scuddling through her.

It had to be fear. It couldn't be excitement.

'You told me last night you'd wait.' Her voice sounded stretched and she tried to conjure calm as panic rose.

Tariq's brows bunched. 'You think I'm about to ravish you?' He looked at their hands locked together, his so much larger and more powerful than hers. 'Is that really what you believe?'

Samira read the stern glint in his eyes and the clamped austerity of his jaw. She'd touched him on the raw.

'I don't know what to think,' she admitted. 'I thought I knew you but I was wrong. You made that clear last night.'

'You knew the boy, not the man.'

He stood proud, unashamed of the man he'd become, the man who'd duped her into believing she was safe with him when all the time he had his own plans. He'd tricked her into believing he'd married on her terms and yet remarkably at this moment she wanted to trust him.

Samira stared up at Tariq. Was he the man she'd known or a stranger? How much had he altered in the years since she'd felt she could trust him with her life?

There'd even been a time, in the distant past, when she'd thought she loved him. He'd been her first romantic crush, the one she'd spent hours daydreaming over with all the fervour of her teenage soul.

Long fingers smoothed her forehead and shivery heat tightened her skin. 'Don't fret about it, Samira.' He paused. 'I have a gift for you. That's all.'

'A gift?' Another one? He'd already presented her with a wealth of exquisite jewellery. Even for a princess born to the opulence of the Jazeeri royal court, her breath had been taken away by his gifts. 'You've given me enough.' She felt overwhelmed by his generosity. Her own gifts, though carefully chosen, weren't nearly as lavish.

'This is something from *me*, not an heirloom.'

There it was again, that glint in his eye that made her shiver. Mentally Samira shook herself. She refused to live her life walking on eggshells.

'That sounds intriguing.'

Tariq's swift, approving smile made her breath catch. He really was stunningly charismatic.

He led her deep into the heart of the palace's private apartments. Samira busied herself admiring the furnishings and the occasional glimpses across the city to the blue smudge of the mountains beyond. Anything to distract her from the intimacy of Tariq's hand enfolding hers, his tall frame imposing yet somehow reassuring as he shortened his stride to match her pace. Being close to him took some getting used to.

Finally they stopped before a wide door. 'After you.'

She pushed it open, only to freeze on the threshold. Slowly, disbelieving, she took in the large, airy space lit by extra-wide, full-length windows.

Samira swallowed, her throat tight, her eyes glazing at the unexpected perfection of it.

'It's wonderful,' she whispered.

'You can go in, you know.'

She hardly heard him. Already she was moving across

the hardwood floor to the massive table in the centre of the room set under powerful lamps. Her fingers trailed the edge of the work surface before moving across to the drawing board, tilted at an angle to catch the natural light. Then to the set of built-in cupboards. The custom-made drawers. The specially designed containers that held bolts of fabric: velvets, silks, lace, satin and chiffon. There was even a mannequin on a podium, again set under brilliant lighting.

Everywhere she looked, in every drawer and corner, was something that pleased her.

Slowly she turned, taking in the careful thought and attention to detail that had gone into making this the ideal work room.

She blinked hard as she recognised the ancient, slightly saggy lounge chair she'd used for the past four years when she'd wanted to curl up and sketch. Beside it was a small wooden table inlaid with mother-of-pearl. It held a sketch pad like the one she always used and a variety of crayons and pencils.

'Your sister-in-law helped me with the details. She sent through photos of your workshop in Jazeer.'

'But this is…' The words stuck in Samira's throat. 'This is far, far better. It's perfect.' She'd never had a custom-made studio. Despite her growing success she'd worked out of a large room she'd adapted in her brother's palace. But this—it was amazing. And it had been created especially for her.

A wave of excitement crashed over her, making her blood tingle. She itched to get to work here.

Samira pivoted to find Tariq just behind her. She grabbed his hand in both of hers, enthusiasm buoying her.

'I don't know how to thank you.' She shook her head, brim-full of emotion. He'd done this for *her*. No gift had

ever been so special, so very *right*. 'Words don't seem
enough.'

'Then don't use words.' His glinting eyes challenged
her, as if he knew she felt over-full, needing an outlet for
the surge of elation and wonder she felt.

Samira's breath hitched in automatic denial, the shut-
ters she'd so carefully built instantly coming up to guard
her from this over-emotional response.

She saw the moment he read the change in her. The moment his gaze altered from challenging to disappointed.

The moment he realised she didn't have the guts to follow through.

When he saw how scared she was.

In that instant the truth blasted her. She had all the
emotions of other women. She felt pain and hope and delight but she'd spent years bottling them up, hiding them
from the world and herself. Because she was scared they'd
make her weak.

She'd let Jackson Brent do that to her.

No, she corrected. She'd done it to herself.

Her nostrils flared in disgust and inadvertently she drew
in the heady spicy aroma of Tariq. It sent a trickle of feminine pleasure coursing through her.

She'd even learned to repress that in the last few years,
hadn't she? She hadn't been interested in a man, much
less turned on by one, in four years. She hadn't let herself.

Suddenly Samira saw herself as Tariq must—wary to
the point of being pathetic.

Was she? Or was she merely cautious? Sensible to protect herself?

But there was a difference between being cautious and
being a coward. Last night she'd been a coward and the
knowledge was bitter on her tongue. All this time she'd
told herself she was being strong. But in reality...

Samira let go of Tariq's hand, instead planting a steadying palm on his hard chest, the other on his shoulder as she rose on tiptoe.

Light flared in those cool eyes but he didn't move, merely stood stock-still, waiting.

She realised she'd stopped breathing and exhaled, then drew in a deep breath redolent of desert spice and hot man. Tariq. His scent enticed. Could he possibly taste as good? Suddenly she had to know.

Samira slipped her hand from his shoulder up to the back of his head, pulling till his mouth was a whisper from hers.

Atavistic warning clawed through her, screaming that she was about to cross a point of no return.

For once, need overrode caution. The need to trust herself, just a little. The need for a man's touch.

Her eyes closed as she pressed her mouth to his. His lips were warm and inviting. She angled her head a little, kissing him again, enjoying his hard body against her, the pleasure of his mouth touching hers.

Samira's other hand snaked up to wrap around his neck, holding him tight as she worked tiny kisses along the tantalising seam of his lips. She felt the exhale of his breath through his nostrils, harder than before, and licked where before she'd kissed. He felt so good. *This* felt so good. If only...

Delicious pleasure hit as he opened his mouth, sucking her tongue inside, drawing her into delight. It was so sudden, so powerfully erotic, that she crumpled at the knees, clinging to his tall frame as his arms wrapped her close.

His mouth worked hers, drawing her to him, delving her depths so she had no option but to surrender that last skerrick of caution.

Samira was captivated. Her whole body came alive in a way she'd never known. Surely no kiss had been like this—a slow kindling that burned bright and satisfying even as it demanded more and yet more?

She arched, moulding herself inch by inch to that strong body she hadn't been able to put from her mind. Still her lips clung to his, hungrier now as his grew more urgent, and a new fire ignited low in her body. Her hands tightened on him. Ripples of heat traced her skin, eddying at her breasts, her pelvis. At her back and hip where he held her so securely.

Her heart was hammering as she tore her lips away, gasping for air. Yet it wasn't lack of oxygen that made her withdraw, but shock at how a thank-you kiss had turned into something completely different. Gratitude and excitement had turned to curiosity, to pleasure and then, almost, to surrender.

She wanted nothing so much as to kiss him again, to lose herself in him.

Samira shivered, suddenly cold despite the hot pulse of blood under her skin. Fear warred with elation.

Tariq still held her, his gaze hooded, waiting, and her stomach churned.

She swallowed, trying to find her voice and not betray rising panic. 'That was…'

His mouth tilted a little at one corner. 'Delightful?' he mused in a low murmur that trawled through her insides, tying her in knots.

'Unexpected,' she gasped.

'A taste of things to come.' His smile deepened, his hold tightening just a fraction.

Instantly Samira stiffened, shaking her head.

She broke from his embrace, staggering back till she came up against the huge work table, her breath coming quick and shallow. Her hands splayed on its edge as she tried to lock her knees. She felt too wobbly to stand alone.

'No.' Her voice was hoarse but she didn't care. She had to make him understand.

She hated that he made her feel weak. She'd taught herself to be strong, hadn't she? She'd taken him by surprise when she'd proposed marriage. She'd been strong then. She refused to cower now.

'No.' Samira locked her hands before her, meeting his eyes directly. 'I told you I don't want love or sex.'

Tariq's teeth bared in a smile she could only describe as hungry. It made her wonder how the graze of his teeth on her skin would feel. 'You say that but your body tells a different story.'

He stepped forward but her outstretched hand stopped him. It took too long for her to realise her fingers had curled into his crisp cotton clothing. She tugged her hand back as if burned.

'Please, Tariq. Believe me when I tell you love is the last thing I want.' Except for the warm, sustaining love between a mother and her children. She'd imagined a special caring too, respect, trust and friendship between husband and wife, but shied from calling it love.

'You made that clear when you proposed. That was one of the reasons I agreed to marry you.'

'It was?' Her eyes widened.

'Definitely.' His gaze shifted, lifting to look past her towards the distant mountains. Instantly Samira felt some of her tension suck away, like a tide suddenly turning. 'The last thing I want is a wife who thinks she's in love with me.' His voice held a honed edge that made her shiver.

Because Tariq was thinking of Jasmin?

Obviously he was. Samira watched his dead gaze as he stared into the distance. She sensed he didn't see the view. It was his first wife he saw. Everyone spoke of how devoted they'd been, how her death had devastated him.

Samira's heart wrenched.

He looked as if a cold wall of steel had crashed down, cutting him off from her. Was his grief still so all-consuming?

Samira wanted to comfort him, except she guessed the last thing he wanted was a reminder that his beloved wife was gone, replaced by a woman he hadn't really wanted.

Suddenly she felt small and unreasonably…hurt.

That was ridiculous. She'd never expected more from him.

Of course Tariq didn't want love. He'd had that from Jasmin and now he couldn't love again. He was a one-woman man. Samira told herself she respected him for that.

He turned and eyes of crystalline green snared her. 'But there's no reason,' he murmured in a low voice of pure temptation, 'why we can't enjoy sex.'

Heat pounded into her. His stare didn't trail suggestively over her body. It didn't need to. It was potent, alight with a desire that made the blood sing in her veins. She struggled to cope with a barrage of sensations as her body responded to that sultry, knowing look. Her emotions jack-knifed from distress to forbidden excitement.

'No. We agreed.'

'You agreed, Samira. I didn't.'

Panic rose anew as she tried and failed to ignore the heat in his eyes and, worse, the answering blaze of hunger in her belly.

It was an aberration.

She threaded her fingers together. 'I told you I don't trust myself with sex and love. I don't—'

'You think sex and love are the same?' His brows crunched together.

'I…' She tilted her chin up. She mightn't have Tariq's vast experience but she had enough. 'For me they are. I never slept with a man I didn't love.' Which meant she'd had one lover and he'd been the biggest mistake of her life. 'Sexual attraction makes you vulnerable. It blinds you to the truth, so you see only what you want to see.' It had been her mother's great weakness and her own. But she'd learned her lesson.

'Oh, Samira.' Tariq shook his head, his hand touching her chin in a fleeting caress that sent shock waves zinging through her. 'You're so inexperienced.'

She huffed out a gasp of mirthless laughter. 'You're the only one to think so.' There was an element of the press, and the public, that insisted on wondering whether she'd been to bed with every man ever photographed with her.

'Believe me, you don't need to be in love to enjoy sex.'

Samira supposed he was thinking of the many beauties who'd warmed his bed before his first marriage and, if rumour was right, in the period since his first wife's death. None had lasted long enough to make a claim on him.

'I know that.' She wasn't a complete innocent. 'But it was like that for me and I can't afford for it to happen again.' She couldn't survive such disillusionment a second time.

'You don't love me, do you?'

'No.' She clenched her jaw.

'Yet you feel this?' *This* was the graze of his knuckles across her breast, lingering at her nipple, making it harden. Her breasts seemed to swell and an arrow of fierce heat shot directly to her womb.

Samira jerked back against the table, shock skittering through her.

'Don't touch me like that!'

'Why not, when you enjoy it?'

She opened her mouth to deny it but he continued. 'I can see the flush of arousal at your throat so don't pretend I'm not right.' His gaze dipped from her neck. 'Your breasts are burning up, aren't they? Is there heat lower too? Deep inside, do you feel empty? Needy?'

Samira gasped as the muscles between her legs clenched

greedily, responding to Tariq's words. He knew her too well. Better than she knew herself.

'I can fill that emptiness, Samira. I can make it good for you. For both of us.'

He could too. Instinctively she knew it. Certainty gleamed in those penetrating eyes. Her body was inching forward, eager for his expert touch.

Samira grabbed hard at the table behind her. 'I don't want that.'

Slowly he shook his head. 'Of course you do. So do I.' His face was taut with a hunger that should have dismayed her, yet instead intrigued her. She imagined them together, here in this room, his big, capable hands gentle yet demanding on her flesh. She wanted…

No! She'd made that mistake once.

'I told you, Tariq, it's not for me. Intimacy and love are bound up together. I won't go there again.'

'You speak with such experience. How many lovers have you had?'

'One.' She jutted her chin. 'That was one too many.'

His gaze narrowed. His words, when they came, held a contained savagery she'd not heard from him before. 'You had your heart broken by a bastard who shouldn't have been allowed even to touch the hem of your dress.'

Samira blinked, taken aback by the depth of Tariq's anger.

'Take it from me, little one, sex can be quite, quite separate to love.' He paused and she sensed he chose his words carefully. 'That makes us an ideal match. I don't want love from you and you don't want it from me. We're on a level playing field. Neither of us will fall for some grand romantic illusion about this marriage.'

Was that bitterness in his voice?

Samira bit her lip. No doubt he was thinking of Jasmin and the fact no other woman could take her place in his heart.

'We have the marriage you wanted,' he continued. 'But we can have more. We can enjoy each other. It's only natural, you know.' This time his touch wasn't at all sexual, a mere brush of fingertips against her hair, yet she felt it all the way to her toes.

'Desire is a part of life. Why not enjoy it? After all, neither of us is in danger of falling in love.'

CHAPTER SIX

A SMILE CURVED Samira's mouth at the way Risay's small hand tucked confidingly into hers as they entered the stables. Shade engulfed them, with the scent of horses, hay and leather.

She paused, letting her eyes adjust, basking in the gentle pleasure of this outing with her new son.

Her son. The word shimmered like a vibration in the warm air, wrapping around her. How long before she grew accustomed to this wonderful new reality?

Her reverie was broken when Risay tugged her hand. Stiff-legged, he marched forward, gabbling in baby language to a man sitting amidst a selection of harnesses.

'Your Highness.' He rose and bowed, a bridle hanging from gnarled hands.

'Please, don't let me interrupt your work.'

With another bow he sat and picked up his polishing cloth. Light from a window caught the ornate silver decorations on the bridle. 'The little prince admires the harness,' he said as Risay strained forward, hand outstretched.

Samira smiled. Anything bright was sure to catch Risay's eye. 'We're looking for the Sheikh. I believe he's here somewhere.'

'Just in the training ring.' The stable hand gestured to the open space on the other side of the building.

The thud of hooves on dirt drew her attention and she

turned to look out of the wide doors. Movement caught her eye.

'I'll look after the young prince if you wish to talk with His Majesty,' the stable hand offered. 'We're old friends.'

Samira dragged her gaze away from the arena. Risay already half-sat on the man's lap, obviously at home, plucking at an intricately wrought harness.

'Thank you.' She nodded and moved towards the open doors.

In a sunlit arena a man and horse faced each other—the horse skittish, its gait high as it pranced, eyes rolling. Her heart jumped as Tariq, unperturbed, approached it. His lips moved and the horse's ears flicked.

Samira's skin drew tight as she caught the delicious, low cadence of Tariq's voice. That same voice had mesmerised her just yesterday.

Desire is a part of life.

Neither of us is in danger of falling in love.

The voice of temptation.

She'd told herself she was immune to such temptation. Yet her body betrayed her. Even here, now, when Tariq wasn't aware of her presence.

Fire trawled her veins, stirred the feminine pulse point between her legs, scorched her breasts. She just had to look at Tariq's powerful frame, hear his rich coffee voice, and she went weak at the knees.

Despair gripped her. Maybe her critics were right. Perhaps she was tainted for ever since she'd once given in to a man's blandishments. Perhaps desire had become an intrinsic weakness, no matter how hard she battled for a cool head.

Her eyes ate him up. He wore a collarless shirt that stuck to broad, muscled shoulders in the heat and pale trousers tucked into boots. Tall, confident and erect as a soldier, he was magnetic. His total lack of fear as the stallion side-stepped wickedly close made her gasp.

Heart in mouth, Samira moved nearer, watching the horse try to intimidate. A rider herself, she understood the stallion's magnificence and the danger. One strike of his powerful hoof could seriously wound.

Yet, as she watched, something changed. That sharply nodding head lowered. Wide nostrils flared as it scented the man who stood, murmuring, keeping eye contact with the big beast.

Seconds strung out to minutes and, apart from quick checks to see Risay was happy, Samira's gaze remained glued on the figure of her husband as he, by some magic, quieted the untamed horse. He didn't even lift his hand, just communed with it in a way she didn't understand.

Finally the horse stepped forward, its gait almost delicate, and blew gustily on his face.

A chuckle sounded in the still air, causing a ripple of sensation deep in Samira's belly. She pressed her hand to the spot, trying to prevent that warm, melting sensation from spreading.

Tariq lifted his hand and the stallion snuffled it. When Tariq turned and moved away, to Samira's amazement, the horse followed like a pet. It nudged his shoulder blade and he laughed, the sound carefree rather than triumphant.

Samira couldn't drag her eyes away. Something inside squeezed tight and hard at the power and pleasure radiating from him. It made her want to reach out and—

'Samira.' He'd seen her. Sensation jolted her as their eyes met.

In swift strides Tariq crossed the arena to stand before her, only a fence separating them.

Despite the breathless clutch of attraction, Samira found herself smiling. 'You have a shadow.'

He turned his head just as the stallion lipped at his shoul-

der. Tariq murmured something she couldn't hear to the
big animal, then, swift as quicksilver, he was through the
fence to stand before her, his eyes keen beneath lazy lids.

Samira breathed him in hungrily, clean sweat and warm
spice. Moisture sheened his forehead and the burnished
skin of his collarbone. Her eyelids flickered as the pulse
between her legs quickened.

'How did you do that?' she asked, needing words to fill
the expectant silence.

'Do what?' His eyes were on her mouth and her nipples
pebbled in anticipation. She shuffled back a step.

'That.' She nodded to the stallion. 'The way you break
in a horse.'

'Ah.' He drew the sound out as he followed her a pace.
Heat beaded Samira's brow. He was too *close*. 'That's the
secret.' He bent his head and his words feathered warm
breath across her face. 'I don't break them. I gentle them.'

His eyes caressed her and she felt it like the graze of
hard fingers along her throat and over her cheek.

She blinked. 'Gentle?' Was he some sort of horse whis-
perer?

'It's a matter of trust,' he murmured in that low voice
with just a hint of gravel. It trawled through her insides,
furrowing pleasure in its wake. 'Once they know I'm not
going to hurt them, they learn to trust.'

The liquid heat in his eyes told her he was talking about
more than horses.

She stiffened. 'You won't hurt them while they abide by
your rules, you mean. You want to be master.' Just as he
wanted to be hers. Disillusionment was still fresh in her
memory. Of how he'd duped her into believing he was safe.

No man had ever looked less safe.

Or more appealing. That was the problem. Her heart
hammered her ribcage as if yearning for her submission.

'You think it's about power?' Slowly he shook his head,

his gaze never leaving hers. 'You had the wrong teacher, Samira.' Heat scorched her skin at his words. They both knew he was referring to her ex-lover. 'It's all about partnership, mutual understanding and enjoyment.'

'Enjoyment?' Instead of disbelief, the single word sounded…needy. She swallowed hard, unable to break away from the enchantment Tariq wove around her with his rich voice and those slumberous eyes that yet danced with anticipation.

'Of course.' He smiled and something hitched in her chest. 'If we don't both enjoy the partnership it won't work.'

Tariq's words hung in the air like a promise. Partnership, enjoyment…was that what he offered where she saw only capitulation and danger?

Samira looked over his shoulder to the dark, glistening eye of the big stallion. Far from being cowed, mischief glinted there. And delight.

Or perhaps her imagination ran away with her. She shook her head, stepping back abruptly to break the spell Tariq wove around her.

Long fingers closed around her hand. His grip was firm but not unbreakable, yet she found herself stilling.

'We're not enemies, Samira.' His tone coaxed. 'We want the same thing.'

She swallowed the words all but bursting on her tongue. Emotionally charged accusations that stemmed from fear, not of Tariq as much as of herself, of this *weakness* she couldn't eradicate but dared not give in to again.

'Risay is here,' she said stiffly. 'Unlike his brother, he refused to settle for a nap without seeing you.'

Tariq's hand loosened around hers as she pulled away, yet even with four whole paces between them the imprint of heat still shackled her.

Then he moved past her in long, easy strides. He hunkered down to Risay's level and weathered his son's enthusiastic embrace with a smile that confirmed what she already knew: that his boys were the light of his life.

He didn't look back over his shoulder at her. His whole attention was focused on his son.

To her dismay, Samira felt excluded. She wanted some of what he gave Risay: his attention, his loyalty. She wanted to bask in his smiles, share his laughter.

And more…so much more.

Laughter rang out, the sound curling around Samira's heart, making her smile. Adil shrieked with joy as his father threw him up and deftly caught him in strong arms. Water droplets caught the dying light as Tariq shook his head. Samira made herself look away. She'd spent too long furtively ogling his powerful body.

This time at the oasis had been far more confronting than the night of their wedding, when Tariq had come to her bedroom and insisted she kiss him. A week had passed and with each day the tension in her had twisted harder.

Her husband stood thigh-deep in the shallows, his swim shorts clinging to powerfully hewn thighs. The sight of him sent Samira's blood pressure hurtling into the danger zone.

She'd never been one to gawk at men. But she'd never spent time with a man like Tariq.

Her one and only lover had been handsome and oh-so-charming, wiry rather than muscular. He'd looked better modelling chic designer clothes than out of them. And she'd discovered that his charm was more often for the camera than for her. Yet here was Tariq, even more appealing in the role of doting father and considerate husband than he was in public.

His eye caught hers and a pulse of awareness passed between them, making her heart beat like a drum. One glance

and instantly she reacted. It had been like that since the
wedding, even though Tariq hadn't pressed her for more.

Each day, each hour, she waited for him to try persuading her into intimacy, only to be *disappointed* when
he treated her with careful courtesy! After their conversation in the stables she'd expected him to make a move
on her, confident of success. Yet he'd let her be. Only the
warmth in his gaze and the way his hand lingered when
they touched proved it hadn't all been a dream. She hadn't
imagined his proposition.

Samira tore her gaze away, kneeling and opening her
arms to Risay as he splashed through the shallows towards her.

The sight of the brilliant smile on his dear baby face
tugged at her heart strings. He and his brother had wel-
comed her into their world with an uncomplicated enthusiasm that reinforced all her fond hopes.

Silently she vowed she'd repay their generosity with all
the love and support they deserved.

Her arms closed around Risay and she snuggled him
close. He was wet and cuddly and chuckled as inevitably
he reached for her hair.

Samira let him play with the knot at the back of her
head. Tiny fingers snagged and pulled. She sighed, acknowledging it was easier to do it herself. With a few swift
movements she released her hair. It tumbled down and
Risay clapped his hands, sitting with a splash in the shallow water, threading his fingers through her long tresses.

'What is it with you boys and my hair?'

'It's the novelty.' Tariq's voice seemed ridiculously
deep after his son's high squeal of pleasure. And it held a
husky note that brushed along her nerves like rich velvet.
'They've never seen anything like it.'

Samira looked up to meet his eyes. There it was again,
that flash of brilliance that made her catch her breath. She

was grateful her hair was loose. It hid the way her nipples swelled against her swimsuit, as if reaching out for his touch. The idea sent discomfort squirming through her.

Yet it was true. Every instinct she possessed urged her to forget her qualms and take what Tariq offered. This honeymoon with him and the twins at the 'small' summer palace on the edge of the desert and the mountains had worn down her doubts and her resistance.

They'd spent almost every waking hour together since he'd set aside royal responsibilities for a week and declared this family time.

It had become appallingly difficult, trying to remember exactly why intimacy with Tariq was such a bad idea when he was with her all the time.

'Sofia, their nanny, has short hair. So do the other staff.'

As he spoke his gaze followed the fall of Samira's hair. That took his stare down to her waist, then lower to the high-cut edge of her swimsuit and her bare thighs. Immediately fire zinged along her veins, concentrating at the sensitive spot between her legs. She shifted her weight and watched a tiny smile tug at his mouth. As if he knew exactly how she responded.

It wasn't the first time he'd seemed to know more about her desires than she did herself.

'Maybe I should get it cut.' Carefully she extricated Risay's fingers from her hair and distracted him with a brightly coloured bucket. 'I've been thinking about it for ages.'

'No!'

Her head swung up at his sharp tone. Tariq was frowning down at her, his game with Adil stopped. What was his problem?

'People cut their hair all the time, Tariq.' It was past time she updated her image. Jackson had suggested it more than once when they'd been together and Samira had worried that her reluctance proclaimed her old-fashioned or just plain cowardly. She'd had long hair all her life. But was that any reason to keep it?

'Please don't.'

Samira opened her mouth to say something offhand, until she read what was in Tariq's eyes and her mouth snapped shut. Heat seared her from top to toe and in every crevice and pulse point in between.

It struck her that this was the first time Tariq had asked her for anything.

She was so distracted she barely noticed Sofia bustling along to gather up the boys and take them back inside for dinner. Slowly Samira stood, stretching her toes to counteract the pins and needles in her feet from kneeling so long. Finding any excuse to look away from Tariq.

But he was still there, still watching, when she straightened. Surely he stood closer?

Her breath stalled. It wasn't just the magnificence of him. Or the fire in his eyes. This was Tariq, the man she'd known and trusted all her life. The man who'd made her dream of a family come true. The man who looked at her and made her feel utterly unlike the sensible, careful woman she'd striven to become.

'Promise me you won't cut it.' Before Samira could work out if that was a request or a command, Tariq reached for her.

He threaded his fingers in her hair, combing slowly from her ear, down past her jaw and throat, hovering for long moments near her breast, then down to where her stomach muscles automatically tensed as he ran out of hair. His hand came to a stop barely grazing the red Lycra at her hip bone.

The hiss of Samira's indrawn breath was loud in the silence. Her muscles clenched hard in response to his feather-light touch. She ordered herself to step back but her legs weren't listening.

'I like it the way it is.' He lifted a fistful of hair and held it to his face, burying his mouth in the dark locks, closing his eyes as he inhaled, his mighty chest rising as if sucking in her essence.

It was the most erotic thing she'd ever experienced. Every erogenous zone in her body slammed into awareness. Samira's mouth dried and her breasts tingled anew. Her knees wobbled alarmingly and she shot out a hand, grabbing his elbow. He felt hot and hard and flagrantly male.

Slowly he lifted his eyes and lightning jolted through her as their gazes met and held.

Could he feel how she shook? Did he hear the rasp of her uneven breathing?

She swallowed hard, telling herself she still had time to retreat. Nothing had happened.

Yet she knew that for a lie. This was... She shook her head. She had no words to describe this.

Tariq stood stock-still. Samira in a red one-piece swimsuit, her sable silk hair rippling in waves to her waist, equalled his most fervid imaginings. The perfume of her skin was in his nose and mouth, like the sweetest of all treats. His lips brushed the impossible softness of her hair and he wasn't sure he could let go.

Yet he'd promised not to rush her. He'd given his word.

This week of holding back from her had almost killed him. His breath sawed in his throat as he struggled to breathe.

He wanted so badly to reach for her. Holding back gouged a chasm through his midriff. But, despite the longing in her eyes, he saw the way her teeth sank into her bottom lip and the tight defensiveness of her shoulders.

Tariq looked into her beautiful face and suppressed a shudder of desire. His need for her was a ravening hunger that obliterated any satisfaction that she was obviously weakening. He'd assured himself it would be easy to enjoy the physical benefits marriage brought. Yet he felt himself hover on the edge of control.

It wasn't supposed to be like *this*. So all-consuming.

Guilt was a sudden sharp, twist of pain driving up from his gut to his heaving chest. How could he feel this rush of powerful desire when not much over a year ago his wife—

He slammed the door on that thought, but not before shame scored him.

Jasmin had asked him to do what was best for the boys, to find a woman who'd care for them as her own. Yet he'd been in no rush to fulfil his promise, appalled at the thought of marrying again. Nothing, he'd thought, would induce him to take another wife, to step into the quicksand that was emotion.

Now, holding Samira's soft hair in his hand, feeling her touch on his arm, he wondered what the hell he'd done. How was he supposed to control *this*?

What he felt was too big, too deep, too raw and unfamiliar. He resented it, despised the weakness it revealed in him. His whole upbringing had been designed to eradicate weakness. His guardian's regimen of hard work, discipline and self-denial had honed Tariq into a man with the strength and single-mindedness to rule a nation, to lead in war if necessary, not to wallow in feelings or succumb to neediness.

Yet his fingers were stiffly reluctant as he released Samira and stepped back. Warm water eddied around his calves. He wished it was deep and icy so he could douse the heat in his blood and his phenomenal erection.

Abruptly he turned, wading out until the water reached his hips and then striking out for the other side of the oasis pool.

CHAPTER SEVEN

TARIQ STOOD, ARM braced high against the open window as he stared at the winking stars. The desert night sky glittered, diamond-bright. A soft breeze feathered across his chest and rippled his loose cotton trousers against his thighs. But it did nothing to cool him. Even the plunge in the oasis and a cold shower later hadn't brought relief from the heat simmering within.

What he needed was a distraction, but the children were in bed and paperwork couldn't hold his attention. Usually it was no effort to work through the evening. But he'd grown so used to Samira's presence, he missed it now. This last week he'd spent most of his time with her, getting reacquainted over a game of chess or backgammon, or discussing the boys. But he'd decided an evening apart was a wise precaution.

A mirthless laugh escaped. He'd planned to accustom her to his presence, use every moment of every day to remind her how good they'd be together and how foolish she was to try denying the inevitable.

How that had backfired!

He was the one so needy he all but climbed the walls with wanting. He was the one who couldn't settle.

He should have made her see reason that first night. Despite her haunted eyes it wouldn't have taken much to seduce her. She was such a sensual woman he could have overcome her doubts in no time.

Now he was paying the penalty for his scruples.

Tariq shoved aside the half-formed suspicion that mere lust shouldn't torture him so. After Jasmin, he knew he was incapable of feeling anything more profound for any woman.

He swung away from the window, intending to dress for a night ride across the desert, when a figure emerged from the shadows near the door.

'Samira!' Even in the gloom she took his breath away. Her long, pale nightdress shimmered with the lustre of a thousand pearls as it shaped her voluptuous form. Her hair lay loosely plaited over one shoulder, trailing down past her breast, lifting with every breath she took.

Tariq swallowed hard, his eyes travelling from her luscious breasts to her tiny waist and the smooth flare of her hips. She moved and a narrow slit revealed one leg all the way to her thigh. He breathed out gustily, trying to rein in his impulse to reach for her and slam her against his body.

'Hello, Tariq.'

'What are you doing here?' He flexed his fingers, then linked them behind his back, away from temptation.

'I want to talk with you.'

Tariq shut his eyes, trying to conjure the willpower he needed. She came to his room dressed like *that* and expected to chat? More and more he wondered just how experienced his bride was in matters of passion.

He'd reached the end of his tether.

'We can talk tomorrow, Samira. It's late.' He strode to the wide bed and dragged back the covers. If that didn't scare her away, nothing would.

Yet she stood her ground. In the dim light he saw her chin jut.

'This won't take long. I know how disrupting a visitor can be just as you're trying to get to sleep.'

Tariq repressed a grunt of laughter. So this was payback for him walking into her room the night of the wedding? If so she had no idea how *disruptive* that had been for him. If she knew she wouldn't have dared venture into the lion's den.

Deliberately he sat on the side of the bed and gestured for her to do the same, knowing she wouldn't.

'Thank you.' To his amazement, she sat down. Not at the far end of the bed, either, but a prim arm's length away.

Tariq took one look at the toned thigh peeping out from her satiny gown and dragged his gaze up to her face. She was tense but more than that he couldn't read in the gloom.

'I wanted to ask you…'

'Yes?' It came out as a growl because inevitably his gaze had dropped again to where she fidgeted with the slit now gaping wide on her thigh. There was only so much temptation a man could withstand.

When she didn't respond immediately he looked up to see her biting her lip.

'Yes?' He managed to sound a little more encouraging.

'How are you sure we can completely separate sex from…' she shrugged and spread one arm wide '…from anything else? How do you know we can keep sex and love separate?'

Tariq felt his pulse pound hard once, twice. He forced himself to sit back, planting his arms behind him on the bed. As if every cell of his being didn't clamour for him to reach for her now. If she'd come this far…

'Bitter experience.'

Her gaze had settled on his chest but now it swung up. 'Because of those other women? Because none of them have been able to fill the gap your wife left?'

'Partly.' The truth was far more difficult and painful. He had no intention of going there. 'I assure you, Samira, love isn't something you need fear from me.' Tariq's mouth twisted at the irony of his situation. If only she knew. 'And your experiences have cured you of that too.'

Slowly she nodded. 'Absolutely.'

'See? It's simple when you think it through. You've already taken a step to build a better life without it. To think with your *head* not your heart.' That was his strength, what he'd been trained to do from birth, eschewing anything that might cloud his judgement. He held out one hand, palm up, on the bed. 'I admire your courage in learning from your mistake and reaching out for what you really want.'

For long seconds she contemplated his outstretched hand. Then, just as his patience frayed, she laid her palm on his. It was delicate and soft, but not weak. He smiled as he folded his fingers around hers.

She was his. Just as he'd planned.

Victory tasted sweet in his mouth. But not as sweet as Samira would be. Already he was salivating, anticipating pleasures to come. He stroked his thumb from her palm up to the pulse point at her wrist and she shivered delicately, her nipples peaking against the clinging nightdress.

'You expect a woman to reach out and take what she wants?' There was a delightful breathless hitch to her voice that awoke a visceral possessiveness in Tariq.

He'd wanted Samira so long. Since the year she'd turned seventeen. Instead of abating, his hunger had intensified with each passing year, torturing him. At first Samira had been untouchable because of her youth and innocence, because of who she was, because their paths lay in different directions. Yet now, against the odds, here she was, his wife.

'Why not?' His voice emerged as a low rumble. 'It's what I'd do.'

His words hung in still air. Then a warm palm planted itself on his chest, fingers splaying as she leaned close. Tariq's breathing faltered. He felt the imprint of her hand right down into what passed for his soul. For a fleeting instant doubt hammered him, the remembrance of all he couldn't offer her.

Then her fingers moved, learning the shape of his body, and doubt fled.

This time it was simple attraction, he assured himself, heady with relief and anticipation. There would be no painful emotional complications.

This time it would be okay.

The knowledge reassured him and fed his arousal.

His eyelids lowered as he fought to rein in rampant hunger to a level that wouldn't panic her. His need was so profound.

'I want you, Tariq.' She whispered the words against his collarbone, pressing a kiss to his burning skin, then another and another, working her way in towards his throat, her mouth soft and hot.

Tariq arched back his head, exhaling with relief and shuddering anticipation. He grabbed her shoulders and with one surging movement hauled her onto his lap, groaning as her satin-clad bounty pressed against him. Her taut backside was on his thighs, his erection nudging her hip, the glorious weight of one full breast in his hand.

Was ever a woman created with the sole purpose of driving a man crazy?

He was near explosion point and they were still dressed. He hadn't felt such urgency since he'd fumbled with his first woman.

Tariq dragged in a breath that smelt of sugary cinnamon with a hint of musk. Sex and Samira, a heady combination.

His mouth found her shoulder and he bit down on the spot that curved up to her neck, knowing how sensitive it would be. The taste of her in his mouth was as heady as he remembered.

She gasped, twisting closer, her breasts thrusting, her

buttocks sliding across his legs. The friction of her hip against his shaft was excruciating pleasure. So was the knowledge that Samira was as aroused as he. She trembled all over as if sensitised to the very weight of the air against her body.

Tariq smiled and sucked gently at the spot he'd nipped. She grabbed his shoulders, fingers digging hard, her breath a low moan that was music in his ears.

'I told you I could make it good for you, Samira.'

But she was past answering. He wasn't even sure she'd heard. Her eyes were slits and her breath came in little pants as she shifted restlessly against him.

To hell with it. Foreplay could wait till the next time. This thing between them was too urgent, too elemental, for games.

He grabbed her waist, the silky material on her delicious body too flagrantly appealing. With a surge of energy he lifted her up to face him, the muscles in his arms locking hard to support her.

'Move your leg over mine,' he growled.

Her eyes opened, looking directly into his, and Tariq felt the impact of her stare thwack him in the chest. He read dazed confusion and a desperation that matched his own.

His arms shook as he lowered her gently onto his lap, pulling her close so her thighs wrapped around his hips. He struggled to breathe in, but the sensation of her heated core hard up against him was almost too much. He gritted his teeth, praying he had the stamina to last.

His hands slipped up her thighs and he found the lace-edged slit on one. Instantly his fingers were under the material, questing over skin every bit as enticing as the delicate, slippery fabric.

She shifted, rising clumsily on her knees, and somehow the silk ripped as his hand plunged higher.

'Sorry.'

For answer she shifted her weight onto one knee, then the other, dragging the material out from under her legs, clearing the way for him. By the time she'd done that he'd yanked open his trousers, freeing himself from the folds of fine cotton.

As she sat back down, Samira gasped and shuddered, her silk-clad breasts exquisitely arousing against his bare torso. Flesh on flesh, heat on heat…the sensations were exquisite torture. He wrapped his arms around her, holding her still against his recklessly pulsing heart.

Did he imagine a flicker of something like anxiety cross her taut features? It couldn't be. It was too late for second thoughts. Yet some part of his almost numbed brain still worked. To his amazement he found himself asking, 'You're sure?'

'Absolutely.' Her voice was that of a temptress, throaty and low. She speared her hands through his hair, clamping his head as she brought her lips to his. Sweet as wild honey, delicious as ambrosia. That was Samira. He plunged into her mouth, demanding complete submission. Elation filled him at her unstinting response. Yet even that wasn't enough.

He let one hand trawl high to the soft hair at the apex of her thighs. It was damp and she jerked at the fleeting brush of his hand. He circled back and she tilted her pelvis greedily, inviting.

An instant later, hands bracing her hips, he lifted her bodily, not breaking their kiss, and positioned her over his erection. She sighed against his lips as he drew her slowly down.

Tariq felt his brain fog, every part of him focused on the sensation of slick pressure as Samira bore slowly down on him. Had there ever been a moment like this? So tight, so perfect, so right?

The taste of her in his mouth, her scent filling his nostrils, the feel of her surrounding him... He shuddered, already too close to the brink.

He devoured her with a marauder's kiss, angling his body higher against hers till she took him all, and ecstasy hovered on the edge of his consciousness.

Samira moaned into his mouth and he swallowed her pleasure, the sound of it rushing through him in fiery trails.

Not yet. Not yet. He wasn't ready to relinquish this.

But there was no holding back. Already he was lifting her high, supporting her as she finally found the rhythm they both needed. Tariq tilted his hips and stroked deep as she returned to him then rose, riding him harder, drawing him in as far as she could.

Fire flashed and her hands grabbed tighter, her movements growing jerky. His blood sizzled, his skin tingling, every sinew and tendon straining as he felt the first ripple of her pleasure drawing him closer to the edge. The ripples became shudders; the synchronicity of their bodies grew staccato, almost out of rhythm. Samira tugged her mouth away, gasping his name as she shattered around him. He'd never heard anything so beautiful.

With a last, desperate surge Tariq powered up hard, touching heaven and spilling himself in spasms of bliss.

A lifetime later he came back to himself. He held Samira tight in his arms: warm and sumptuous. Her thighs locked around him, her body trembling, each movement teasing him with agonised delight.

Tariq breathed slowly, filling burning lungs. His brain still swam. He felt dazed, as if he'd passed through some mysterious rite of passage.

He frowned, unsettled at the way something at once familiar could feel so extraordinary.

Samira snuggled closer, her breathing muffled in his collarbone, wetness smearing his shoulder.

'Samira?' He wouldn't have known his own voice. It

was a hoarse, unfamiliar rasp. 'Are you crying?' Dismay rose at the suspicion that glorious, white-hot sex had turned to something else. Something fraught with female emotion.

She shook her head. The movement brushed her breasts against his chest and Tariq sucked in his breath as pleasure stirred anew.

'It's just a little overwhelming.'

'Good overwhelming?' He found himself soothing her back with gentle, circular strokes.

'Fantastic overwhelming.' She sniffed and blinked, her wet eyelashes spiky against him. 'I've never done it like that before.' Her head tipped up and huge, soft eyes met his. He knew an insane urge to fall into those glowing depths and lose himself for ever. 'Is that why it was so amazing?'

Tariq felt his eyes widen. She'd never had sex astride a man? It was hardly adventurous sex. Hastily he began revising his assumptions about her level of experience. It seemed that her famous ex-lover, despite his notoriety, had left Samira remarkably inexperienced.

Tariq couldn't stop his hands from skimming up her sides to brush the edges of her breasts. Her jump of pleasure and her startled stare, as if surprised at her body's response, told its own story.

'No, that's not why it was amazing. It's just us, Samira. The chemistry between us.'

And the fact that she'd been in his blood for over a decade. No wonder his orgasm had been so explosive.

He felt the sudden tension in her and knew at once she was second-guessing the implications.

'Good sex is like that, Samira. It's nothing to fret over.'

Finally Samira dropped her head onto his shoulder, slumping sated against him. He rested his chin on her head, feeling the tickle of her hair, the softness of her body against him, her tight, enticing heat.

And as easily as that he was ready again, heavy with arousal, deep inside her.

Samira's indrawn breath said it all.

Shock hammered him even as he moved tentatively, wresting a sigh and a little shiver of pleasure from her. Her lips pressed to his shoulder, her tongue swiping his damp flesh.

In all these years he'd never wanted any woman as much as he wanted Samira.

Nothing in his past compared with his passion for her.

Tariq swallowed an iron-hard knot of guilt but couldn't dispel the shame in his belly or the burn of desire.

He'd never wanted Jasmin like this.

That was significant enough.

But it was more than that. The truth stripped him of honour, eating into his corroded soul.

He felt more for Samira after a week than he'd felt for his first wife after four years of marriage.

What kind of man was he?

CHAPTER EIGHT

THE REMAINS OF the village were a pathetic mess, even after a team of engineers and builders had been hard at work. Samira struggled to keep her eyes on the faces before her, rather than stray past them to the pitiful rubble, the ruins of what had once been homes clinging to the edge of the narrow valley.

She swallowed hard. She'd never seen such devastation.

Yet the women around her in the new community centre were beaming, excited to welcome their queen. They'd turned the building, currently used for emergency accommodation, into an inviting space, like the interior of the vast nomad tents their forebears had used. Rugs lined the floor and walls and sweet treats were proffered on platters.

Tariq had been right. Her presence today, wearing sumptuous traditional dress rather than the more sombre outfit she'd planned, had been the distraction these women needed. And his insistence that they bring the boys had been a masterstroke.

Samira smiled and thanked the young girl with huge eyes who offered her tea in a tiny, filigree-edged glass. The girl ate up everything about her from her scarlet silk skirts to her old gold jewellery and henna-stained hands.

With their backs to the open doors, older women sat beaming, clucking over Adil and Risay as they played with a couple of local toddlers in the safety of the circle of adults. Some women wore traditional finery, silver coins

sewn into their scarves, their dresses trimmed with exquisite embroidery, bangles clinking on their arms. Others,
whom Samira guessed had been lucky to survive the flash
flood that had swept away half the village, wore plainer
garments. But even they were smiling.

Samira sipped the tea, declared it delicious and turned
to her nearest neighbour. Conversation was tentative at
first, but grew animated as the women lost some of their
shyness. Their talk centred on the recent devastation and
plans to rebuild.

Opinion was unanimous that the recovery effort had
been wonderful. Why, the royal Sheikh himself had been
here the day after it had happened! He'd taken a personal
interest in the rebuilding, insisting the plans be developed
in consultation with the community.

The Sheikh was so capable. So wise. So willing to listen.
So handsome.

A titter of laughter circled the room and all eyes focused on Samira.

To her amazement she felt heat wash her cheeks, just as
if she were a real bride besotted with her husband.

She wasn't besotted. But she *was* a bride. Ever since
the night she'd found the courage to face her fear and her
desire for Tariq and gone to him, she'd been swept up in a
world of sensual pleasure and breathless anticipation. Life
had never felt so…real, so vibrant and exciting.

Her gaze shifted outside to where Tariq, wearing jeans,
boots and a hard hat, clambered with a group of men over
rubble beside the scaffolding for a new building.

Predictably her mouth dried as she took in his towering
form. Broad-shouldered, slim-hipped, long-legged, he was
so masculine just the sight of him did funny things to her.

And the memory of the things he did with her in the
privacy of their rooms… Her blush intensified, to the delight of the women around her.

She smiled and shrugged, accepting their gentle ribbing with good grace. Why shouldn't she? She had it all. The children she'd craved, the husband who respected but didn't try to dominate her. And sex that could melt her bones, nights of glorious pleasure that left her feeling better than she ever had in her life.

What more could she want?

Tariq turned, following the gestures of the village elder and project manager as they discussed how the new site for the village was so much safer than the old one. They'd been over this before and his attention strayed to Samira sitting surrounded by women in the newly constructed community centre. Even from this distance he saw the stiff formality of the group had disappeared, replaced by what looked and sounded like a party.

A grin tugged his mouth as he heard laughter and saw an old woman pick up Adil and croon to him. It would do his sons no harm to get out of the palace and be with his people. Their people. Learning to mix with strangers would stand them in good stead for the future.

But it was his bride who drew his eyes.

From the moment she'd emerged in her finery this morning he'd wanted to bundle her back into her bedroom and strip away the gossamer silk that made her shimmer like some enticing gift waiting to be unwrapped. Or maybe it was the knowing glint in those warm, sherry eyes, reminding him of how they'd spent the better part of the night, naked and desperate for each other.

Even now, with the whole population of the village between them, he felt his blood rush south, his groin tighten as need stirred.

He found himself striding towards the village centre, the men following.

There was a stir among the women as they made ready

to serve refreshments to the men. He was given the place of honour, the headsman to his right, Samira to his left. He breathed in her sweetness and looked down, registering the slow-fading henna on her hands that marked her as his. Once more Tariq felt a surge of triumphant possessiveness.

As ever, it sideswiped him. Such intensity, such need, was unprecedented.

Black guilt hovered as it had after they'd had sex the first time. With it came a frisson of warning, as if someone stroked an icicle down his spine. A sense that with Samira he'd strayed into unknown, dangerous territory.

Tariq wrenched his mind free before the thought could take hold.

He had exactly what he wanted. Life was good. So good that for the first time since boyhood he toyed with the idea of cutting short his official duties to escape and enjoy himself.

Tariq exhaled slowly and forced himself to focus. He had responsibilities, duties. He was totally in control of the situation no matter how wayward his thoughts. He would keep everything in perspective, including his desire for his wife.

Tariq snared her wrist as they entered the royal apartments. 'Let Sofia put the boys down for their nap.'

'But it's no trouble. I like doing it.' Samira's confidence with them grew each day, and they had accepted her into their lives.

She'd done the right thing, proposing this marriage. The niggle of doubt that she'd tied herself to a man who'd tricked her, pretending to accept her terms, then breaking down her resistance to sex—well, it was only a niggle. After all, she enjoyed this marriage with benefits as much as he.

She'd been naive believing they could live together celibately. But in everything else, he'd been honest with her. Of course he had. This was Tariq. The man she'd known all her life.

'Leave them.' His voice was a low burr that burrowed to the core of her. 'You can do it tomorrow.'

She met his hooded stare and nodded, trying to dispel the heated blanket of awareness that engulfed her whenever he was near.

Sitting beside him at the village reception had been torture. The whole time she'd smiled and made polite conversation her skin had been drawn too tight, her blood pulsing too fast, her body crying out for his touch.

It had taken him no time at all to persuade her into intimacy. Persuade! She'd all but jumped him, once she'd accepted his assurance that intimacy and love could be separate.

And now... She gulped, watching his eyes darken. Now she struggled to pretend she didn't spend all her time thinking about him. She'd opened the Pandora's box of sexual closeness and was more in thrall to Tariq than she could ever have expected. Her breathing sharpened. With fear or excitement?

'We need to talk about today.' He turned abruptly towards their private corridor.

Talk? She stifled disappointment. 'Of course. I thought it went well. Did you?'

'Better than expected. Everyone sounded positive despite what they've been through.' Yet Tariq's words didn't ring with satisfaction. She caught an undercurrent of urgency in them and wondered what was wrong.

Samira hurried to keep up with his lengthening stride.

'They appreciate all you're doing. The women kept singing your praises.' A blush rose at the memory of their enthusiasm, the compliments for her fine husband who was not only strong but handsome and no doubt virile. 'You won their trust early, going there in person at the time of the emergency and helping with the rescue mission.'

Her pride in him swelled. Tariq was an outstanding leader, hands-on as well as strategic, not one who only sat back and supervised at a distance. His presence had brought real hope to the villagers.

'They're my people. Where else would I have been?'

He led the way into the first of their private sitting rooms but, instead of halting by the cluster of comfortable chairs, Tariq closed the door behind them, then strode on.

'Didn't you want to talk?' There was a breathless catch in her voice as she scurried to match his pace.

'Is that what I said?' The look he slanted her sizzled all the way to her toes.

Swiftly he turned. In her traditional flat slippers she felt tiny against his towering bulk. His shoulders blocked out the room and she had to tilt her neck to hold his gaze as a thrill of anticipation shot through her. She'd never felt so overwhelmingly feminine as with Tariq.

'What I *want*...' the rough texture of his voice weakened her knees '...is to be alone with you as soon as possible.'

His hands were on her, lifting her against a pillared archway. Shocked, she opened her mouth to speak but instead her breath came out in a gasp of satisfaction as he pressed close, his torso to her breasts, his powerful thighs hard and insistent, pushing hers apart.

Samira roped her arms around his neck, holding tight, reeling as a wave of desire crashed over her, threatening to drag her under. His solid heat inflamed her. An urgent throb of need pulsed at the spot where he wedged himself close, taking her from zero to boiling point in mere seconds. Even the tang of desert heat and male spice tickling her nose was arousing.

'The bedroom is just there,' she whispered, shimmying higher in his arms, pushing against his hard shaft, unmistakeable through the fine silk of her dress. Tariq's unashamed arousal and his urgent passion were a continual revelation.

As was her inevitable response.

It struck her anew how very controlled Jackson's lovemaking had been. Surely she shouldn't feel so *driven* by the need to have Tariq right here, right now, as if nothing mattered except having him inside her?

When had she become so wanton?

'You think I can last till the bedroom?' Tariq groaned and bent his head to bite her neck. Samira shuddered as pleasure ripped through her, turning her body molten.

Everything in her softened. Breasts, belly, womb all hummed with the need for more. Her hands tightened, grabbing handfuls of his thick hair, holding him hard as he kissed the sensitive skin of her throat.

'Hold on.' He moved, pressing her up against the wall. She heard the chink of his belt buckle, felt him fumble between them. Then he was fighting his way past her long skirts, shoving the silk up her legs till she felt a waft of air on her bare thighs.

She almost slipped but big hands hoisted her higher, guiding her legs till they encircled his waist. And all the time his eyes held hers. It was as if she hovered on the brink of diving into a fathomless mountain pool.

Except it was heat she felt as he ripped her panties away and she gasped with horrified delight. Pure fire she touched as with one sure thrust Tariq embedded himself deep within her.

She was so incredibly full, as if he stretched her to the limit. As if they'd become one, she thought hazily as he retreated, then thrust hard again, creating ripples of delight that took her straight to the edge. She grabbed tight, needing this oneness with him.

'Samira.' He ground the word, his jaw hard, his hands

heavy on her body. She revelled in his touch and moved eagerly with him. He paused, then surged again, taking her to new heights. 'You have no idea how I hunger for you.'

She tried to gulp in enough air to catch her breath. 'I do.' It made her desperate, this unquenchable need for her husband. But the more she gave, the more she trusted him, the stronger it grew. 'I want you all the time,' she gasped.

He stilled and she almost cried out in frustration. Till she registered his expression. She couldn't interpret it, but those eyes gleamed more brightly than ever. As if they could burn right through her.

When he stroked again, he took her to heaven's door. The world burst into fireworks. Through a haze of bliss she just caught his words.

'I've always wanted you, Samira. Always. And now you're mine.'

Samira lay sprawled across Tariq on the bed, her limbs dissolved, her head on his heaving chest. His heart hammered beneath her ear, rapid like hers. Her palm rested on his chest, fingers furrowed into the smattering of hair that she still found so intriguing.

'I don't think I can walk,' she whispered.

She felt more than heard his huff of laughter. 'Good. I don't want you going anywhere.' He pulled her closer, as if just the thought of her moving wasn't to be considered.

Samira smiled sleepily. She'd lost her shoes when he carried her here and her dress was twisted around her hips but she didn't have the strength to move. His breath was hot on her face and his hand played languidly with her hair, loose to her waist. She felt...replete. As if there was nowhere she'd rather be. Not in her work room. Not even with the twins.

'I like that you're so strong.' She rubbed her face against his skin, inhaling that delicious scent: essence of Tariq.

'The way you held me back there…' Just thinking about it made her inner muscles clench in remembered pleasure. Samira adored it when Tariq's loving was slow and thorough but hard and fast definitely had a lot to recommend it.

'I like that you're so eager for me.' She heard the smile in his voice and imagined his smug grin. No wonder. He'd overturned her 'no sex' rule in mere days and now she couldn't get enough of him.

It was just sex, of course. Sex and liking. A marriage with benefits.

Yet his earlier words lingered in her mind, teasing her.

'What did you mean—you've always wanted me? Since the day I came to you in Paris?'

Tariq said nothing. His fingers dragged through her hair, making her head tilt up. From here she saw his solidly hewn jaw and the strong column of his throat as he swallowed.

'Tariq?'

'Since then too. When you came to the hotel in that tight skirt and jacket I wanted to rip them right off you.' His fingers strayed across to her hip, distracting her as he traced delicate whorls of pleasure on her flesh.

Samira wriggled and clamped her hand on his, making him stop.

'Since then *too*? What does that mean?'

He sighed. 'You always were tenacious, weren't you?'

She'd had to be. If she'd waited for her parents to give her guidance she'd have waited all her life. She'd had to cling to her dreams, forging her career despite the roadblocks: disbelief that a princess actually wanted to learn to sew; prejudice from peers, teachers and the public who thought she wasn't serious or that she'd pulled strings to get her sought-after training place.

'It's not a trick question, Tariq. What did you mean?'

'What I said. I've always wanted you.'

The words shimmered in the air, simple yet devastating. Samira blinked, trying to get her head around them.

'Define "always".'

'You're not going to let it go, are you?' He lifted his head and fixed her with a stern eye. She stared back. He might be the Sheikh of Al Sarath but she was his wife. She had a right to know.

Tariq let his head drop back on the pillow. Beneath her hand his fingers resumed their leisurely exploration of her hip.

'I've wanted you for years. Since you were seventeen, to be precise,' he said at last, effectively stealing her voice. Samira's heart fluttered.

'I remember coming to Jazeer that winter as usual. My uncle encouraged me to learn as much as possible about our neighbouring states.' Silently Samira nodded. Tariq's stern uncle had been his guardian till Tariq had come of age. He'd raised his orphaned nephew along with his own much younger sons. She'd often thought that was why Tariq had been so patient with her. How many boys and young men put up with their best friend's kid sister following wherever they went?

But wanting her since she was seventeen? She felt like someone had upended her world, leaving it altered for ever.

At seventeen Samira had been increasingly aware of Tariq, not just as her brother's friend but as the sort of man a teenage girl could hang her dreams on: those dreamy eyes; the deep, smooth voice that did strange things to her insides and still did. That tough, lean body.

Her younger self had been embarrassed and excited by the new daydreams she'd begun to have about him. She'd even wondered if she'd given herself away and that was why he'd left so abruptly, never to return.

'I never suspected,' she said at last.

'Of course not. That would have been unforgivable. You were my best friend's sister. And you were far too young. You weren't meant to know.'

Samira frowned. 'Never?'

What if she'd known years ago that Tariq had been attracted to her? She'd spent long enough mulling over her mistakes to know her infatuation with Jackson Brent had stemmed as much from self-doubt and her need for love, as from his attractiveness and his efforts to charm her.

Despite her looks, perhaps because of them, Samira had always harboured a fear she was fatally flawed, all show and no substance. Maybe because her parents had never really cared for her, she'd always secretly believed she was unlovable. Hence her reckless leap into a relationship with the first man to sweep her off her feet.

Knowing that a man she respected, like Tariq, was attracted to her... Could that have changed her attitude and given her a little more confidence?

Or was that wishful thinking?

'You were untouchable, Samira. It wouldn't have been right. That's why I left.'

Had he really wanted so badly to touch her? There was something in his voice, an echo of regret that resonated deep.

Samira twisted, lifting her head to look at his face. His forehead was corrugated, his mouth set in a firm line.

'You left because of me?' A flurry of emotion hit her—regret, dismay and delight.

Tariq raised one arm, slipping his hand beneath his head. His biceps bulged, a reminder of his latent power. Heat streamed through her all over again. She blinked, distracted by the urgent flutter of response in her belly.

'What else could I do? I felt guilty, lusting after a kid who looked on me as a big brother.' His tone was hard.

'But you stayed away. You never came back.'

Tariq shrugged. 'It was better that way.'

What he left unsaid was that by the time she'd grown he'd lost interest, for he'd never returned. Instead she'd heard the rumours of his many lovers. Then he'd married Jasmin, whom everyone said was the love of his life. Of course he'd never have come back. Samira must have been a passing fancy. Given his distinction between sex and love, she could only guess he'd lost his heart to his first wife and knew no one could replace her.

He'd made no secret that first day in Paris that he hadn't wanted to marry. Because he still loved Jasmin? Samira had assumed so. But now, in Tariq's bed, the idea tore at something deep inside. Her chest squeezed as an ache filled her.

Had he married her out of pity?

Samira bit her lower lip and looked away, subsiding against his chest.

No. Not pity. The way Tariq touched her didn't feel at all like pity.

He wanted her physically. What they shared was simple and mutually satisfying. Now she had a family, a place to belong, real purpose. The boys were bonding with her and hopefully would come to love her. Tariq respected her. Plus there were the benefits of sex.

Why then did dissatisfaction grate at her? Why the bitterness on her tongue, the edge of disquiet?

Samira breathed deep, inhaling the musky man aroma she'd come to adore, and forced herself to relax. Automatically Tariq curled his arm around her, drawing her close, his breathing slowing beneath her ear.

She had everything she wanted, she reminded herself. More, given the glow of wellbeing in her sated body and heavy limbs.

Yet Tariq had unsettled her. His revelation made her realise she didn't know him as well as she'd thought. All these years she'd been certain of two people in her life: her brother, Asim, and his best friend, Tariq.

Now Tariq made her question what she thought she knew.

First had come the revelation he'd misled her, pretending to accept a paper marriage. Next the revelation she'd never known him as well as she'd thought. All those years ago he'd hidden how he felt from her.

Had she known him at all?

Surely the decent, caring man she'd known hadn't been a mirage? She saw him in the man Tariq had become.

But there was another side to her husband. He wasn't just a gentle giant. He was a virile, clever, powerful man who got exactly what he wanted.

What did he want from her?

She'd assumed he'd married her to acquire a mother for his children, a consort.

That and a sexual partner.

It couldn't be anything else. Despite their sizzling passion, Tariq always left her to sleep alone. He respected her privacy. He gave her the distance she wanted. He didn't demand an *emotional* bond.

Because she wasn't the wife he'd chosen for himself. Samira sighed, realising her thoughts had come full circle, back to Jasmin.

Tariq might share himself now with Samira, but he'd never love her because Jasmin held his heart.

Samira had understood that from the first. Why, then, did the knowledge dim her incandescent glow of pleasure?

Why did she feel so...lost?

CHAPTER NINE

'ALLOW ME TO congratulate you on your lovely bride. You've chosen well, my friend.'

Tariq followed the direction of the old Emir's gaze, though he knew what he'd see. Despite having been married for months now, his attention kept straying to the far side of the reception room, to his wife. As if he couldn't get enough of her. Samira glowed, her skin peach-perfect, her delicious body ripe and even more voluptuous than when they'd married. Those luscious breasts seemed fuller, more pert than ever.

He forced his attention elsewhere but his eyes snagged on the alluring curve of her smile, her graceful gestures.

Pride swelled. Samira was a superb hostess.

She chatted easily with guests: diplomats, VIPs and... Tariq noted a familiar handsome face and blond hair, the project manager overseeing the rebuilding project in the mountains. Nicolas Roussel hung on her every word. Samira took such an interest in the project that every time Tariq turned around Roussel was at her side.

Just as well Tariq knew she wasn't interested in any man but himself.

'Thank you.' He nodded, acknowledging the Emir's compliment. 'I count myself fortunate.'

For she didn't just excel at social events. Samira was also a caring queen. Her personal gift of sewing machines and bolts of fabric, sent to women in the flood-ravaged mountain villages, had been just right. It had lifted their spirits, as well as given them a potential source of income. She'd even commissioned fine embroidery from them for use in her designs and had laid the groundwork for a successful local enterprise.

'I admit I wondered about a queen who runs her own business.' The old man shook his head, raising his hand when Tariq would have spoken. 'But I stand corrected. It seems to me that your wife's experience as an entrepreneur gives her a broader view of the world. My wife and I have enjoyed her company during our visit. And,' he chuckled, 'my daughter is smitten with the gown your wife designed for her. She's a very talented woman.'

Tariq inclined his head. The Emir, ruler of a neighbouring state, was notoriously conservative and his good opinion hard-won. Samira had done well to impress him.

'I believe so.'

'It was sensible of you to lose no time providing a mother for those boys of yours. I hear she dotes on them. No doubt she's getting broody about having some of her own too, eh? It shouldn't be long.' He winked.

Tariq stiffened. The old man didn't say anything others weren't thinking. Yet Tariq remembered Samira's pale features as she'd told him she could never have children. Her pain had dragged at him like a plough scraping through rough soil.

'We're content as we are,' he said through tight lips.

'No need to poker up about it. I've seen the way you look at her. The pair of you can barely keep your eyes off each other. You're obviously both besotted.' He clapped an arm on Tariq's shoulder. 'You're a red-blooded man with a beautiful wife. Make the most of it.' He turned his head. 'Ah, I see I'm wanted. If you'll excuse me?'

Tariq had to work to keep his face bland as the older

man moved away. The Emir had rattled him more than he'd thought possible.

Besotted? Hardly. He was incapable of such unguarded emotion. That was a strength he'd accrued from his strict, unsentimental upbringing. There'd been no room for love in his formative years, no soft, feminine influence. It was only later he'd learned such invulnerability was also a flaw.

When he'd discovered Jasmin, carefully chosen for their arranged, dynastic marriage, loved him.

It had been unexpected, unwanted. Terrible.

For, no matter how much he respected and admired her, Tariq hadn't been able to return those feelings.

His mouth thinned. Samira had been adamant she didn't want romantic love. Perhaps he should have come straight out and told her he was incapable of it. If he'd been able to fall in love it would surely have been with Jasmin. She'd been gentle, loyal and hard-working, deserving of love. And he'd seen how she'd suffered when her feelings weren't returned.

He'd tried so hard and failed abysmally. She'd never won his heart, leaving him to conclude that, like his upright but emotionally isolated uncle, he didn't have a heart to win.

He'd done his best to make it up to her in attentiveness. But it hadn't been enough. He'd seen it in her eyes.

Tariq had failed her. The knowledge ate at him like a canker. Despite his wealth and power he hadn't been able to save Jasmin's life. Nor had he been able to give her the one thing she'd craved—love.

Abruptly Tariq turned his back on the group surrounding Samira, his heart pounding.

The Emir was mistaken. Samira didn't want love. She'd married him for his sons.

And he... He wanted her, craved her. He'd craved her even when she'd been with another man. Even when he'd been married to another woman.

So much for being a man of honour!

A chance sighting of a press photo of Jazeer's scandalous princess had been enough to send him into a lather of activity, extending his already full schedule in an attempt to work off desires he had no right feeling. Guilt had driven him to be the ideal husband to Jasmin in every way left open to him.

Tariq breathed deep. The past was past. He'd done the best he could for Jasmin. And as for wanting Samira—she was his wife now. Why shouldn't he desire her?

They had the perfect marriage. Respect. Affection. Phenomenal sex. But no illusions of love.

'Risay, you're becoming such a big boy.' Samira smiled encouragingly as he tackled the long noodles in his bowl, amazed at how he'd grown in the months since the wedding.

Beside him Adil was absorbed in pulling the pasta apart and dropping it from his high chair. He caught Samira's eyes, picked up another thread of pasta, then let it fall, crowing with delight as it hit the floor. Samira laughed. 'And you, Adil, are going to be a charmer with that cheeky smile and those big green eyes.'

Just like his father. No one would call Tariq cheeky, but his smile made her heart flip over. It transformed his face from austere to stunningly charismatic. Every time she saw it Samira's breath caught beneath her ribs.

She shifted in her seat. Strange that she had that slightly breathless feeling now, as if carrying the boys down the corridor and putting them in their high chairs was more effort than before.

'Is everything all right, madam?'

Samira smiled up at Sofia who'd just appeared with the boys' juice cups. 'Yes, thanks. Just getting a bit more comfortable.'

She tugged at the fabric of her skirt that had bunched high when she sat. How could the waistband need adjusting again?

She'd got in the habit of wearing loose dresses in private, but she'd been with a client today and had put on a narrow tailored skirt and jacket of peacock-blue in the retro fifties style Tariq appreciated so much. Probably because of the way it clung to her hips and thighs.

Samira frowned. Maybe she should give up wearing it until she slimmed down. She hadn't noticed herself eating more but clearly Tariq's excellent royal chefs were having an impact. If she didn't do something soon to get back in shape she'd be as fat as butter.

'Are you sure nothing's wrong, madam?'

'Nothing at all. Just a little too much good food.'

Sofia nodded and clucked her tongue as she removed Risay's empty bowl. 'Fitted clothes like that will get more difficult to wear. You'll be more comfortable in traditional dresses and loose trousers from now on.'

Samira sat straighter, surprised at the nanny's readiness to discuss her employer's weight. None of the servants at home in Jazeer would have dreamed of making it obvious they'd noticed.

'I didn't mean to offend, madam.' Sofia must have seen her surprise. 'It's only natural, though it does take some getting used to.' She patted her own narrow waist and Samira stared, perplexed.

'I'm sorry. You've lost me. What takes getting used to?' Samira stood up, ready to lift Risay from his chair.

'The way pregnancy changes your body. It can seem overwhelming the first time.'

For a heartbeat Samira stared, stunned, then her arms dropped to her sides, leaden weights. She'd expected this sort of speculation but still it was discomfiting.

'I'm afraid you're mistaken.' Deliberately she shaped

her lips into a casual smile. 'I'm not pregnant.' She would have to school herself to say it without sounding quite so hollow.

'You're not?' Sofia looked taken aback. 'I'm so sorry. I could have sworn... I've never been mistaken before. And you have the look.'

Despite herself Samira was curious. Her one experience of carrying a child had been over almost before she'd realised it. She'd never had regular periods and hadn't had any obvious symptoms so she'd been blithely unaware of the baby she carried. There had barely been enough time to adjust to the wondrous news before the trauma of losing it.

'There's a look?' She couldn't help asking, though she knew she shouldn't torment herself by prolonging this.

Sofia nodded emphatically. 'You've got it. There's a look in the eyes, and your skin glows, and...' She stopped, her gaze sliding away.

'And?'

Sofia shrugged. 'You've gained a little weight. Not only in the waist but here too.' Her hands plumped up her own breasts.

Suddenly Samira found herself sitting, her head spinning.

No. It was completely far-fetched. It was impossible.

And yet...

She bit her lip, admonishing herself for even that brief flight of fancy. There was a world of difference between wishful thinking and reality. She'd made it her business to live in the real world, not pine for what could never be.

She crossed her arms, then immediately dropped them at the graze of fabric over her nipples.

'Sensitivity there too.' Sofia added helpfully, as if reading her discomfort.

'I—' Samira shook her head. She would *not* go there. Her breasts had been sensitive for some time, but she couldn't tell the other woman it was because of the attention Tariq devoted to them. If he wasn't caressing her breasts with his hands, he had his mouth on them, knowing it drew exquisite pleasure from her. Her nipples tingled as she remembered the attention he'd lavished on them last night, and on every other part of her body.

Her breath sucked hard.

'Thank you for your concern, Sofia, but I'm afraid you're mistaken.' She stood briskly and began to help the nanny clear the boys' food away.

But, as she put the twins down for their nap, Samira couldn't shake the memory of Sofia's certainty. Samira's grandmother had prided herself on her uncanny ability to spot a pregnancy. She'd claimed it was a gift and that in all her decades she'd never been wrong.

Was Sofia also gifted with such insight?

If she was, she was badly mistaken this time.

Samira looked down at the boys, already drowsing after their busy day, and found her hand had crept unbidden to her stomach. It wasn't just her waist that thickened. Her belly curved out now too. Yet, though she'd always had a curvy figure, Samira had never had weight problems.

She bit her lip, trying to force down the tremulous hope that rose like a tiny green shoot in an arid desert.

The anguish of losing her tiny infant, and of hearing she'd never conceive again, was a raw wound in the darkness of her psyche. She couldn't afford to reawaken that pain with false hope.

Yet as she left the bedroom she found herself wondering.

Samira slumped down onto the side of the marble bath, staring at the test result. Her fingers shook so much she told herself she wasn't reading it right.

She pressed her palm against her abdomen as if she

could feel anything new there. Or as if the touch of her hand could protect the new life sheltering within.

Panic slammed into her. She hadn't been able to protect the baby she'd carried four years ago. How could she this time?

Nature hadn't wanted her to be a mother. Hadn't she been told she wouldn't conceive again?

Her skin tightened. Her forehead and the back of her neck prickled, turning clammy with the cold sweat of fear.

The test indicator clattered to the floor as Samira's vision hazed with nightmare memories. Blood and pain and the devastatingly gentle tone of a stranger telling her it was too late, she'd lost her child.

Instinctively Samira pressed her legs together so hard they grew numb. She blinked back the hot tears glazing her eyes and forced herself to think. She'd hunched over into a foetal position, body bowed and knees drawn up to protect the new life inside.

Her breath hissed, loud in the silence. She carried a new life!

She was pregnant. Against the odds she was pregnant.

And if one miracle could happen—her conceiving again—perhaps it was possible another miracle might happen and her child would be born alive and healthy.

Samira gulped over the burning ball of emotion in her throat.

If she'd learned one thing it was never to give up. She'd dragged herself from the darkest of places after the grief and scandal of her past. She refused to go back to living in the shadows.

Gingerly she straightened, taking stock of how she felt.

A smile hovered. She felt fine. More than fine, she felt fit as a fiddle, except for the way nerves made her stomach roil.

She breathed deep, then bent to pick up the test result, her fingers closing tight around it.

It could be a false positive. Gravely she nodded to herself as if she actually believed that. As if excitement wasn't skittering through her, as if her blood wasn't fizzing with elation and her toes curling.

What she needed was certainty, a doctor.

Again she nodded. Good, she was thinking clearly and logically.

Yet when Samira stood up she saw that the woman facing her in the mirror wore a smile so broad it could only be described as rapturous.

Tariq paused midstride and stared at the retreating back of the man following one of the maids at the far end of the corridor. An icy hand clamped his neck.

No, he was mistaken. It was a trick of the light. The obstetrician had no reason to visit the palace.

Yet Tariq was blindsided by memories of the last time he'd seen that doctor. Tariq had been hollow with shock, unable to believe the world had turned on its head. He'd been given his precious sons but at the cost of Jasmin's life. Joyful expectation had turned to disaster.

He'd grappled with the unnerving sense that he'd lost control. All his wealth and influence hadn't been able to save Jasmin. In fact, his need for an heir had caused her death.

Shaking off fraught memories, he continued on, opening the door to the royal suite and striding in. He wanted Samira. Just being with her made him feel good. How corny was that? Her warmth and understanding, her company, were as essential to him now as her physical generosity.

After that moment in the corridor, when dark tendrils from the past had wound around him, squeezing so he couldn't breathe, he needed Samira.

She wasn't in her room but he heard water running in her bathroom. His step quickened.

'Samira?' He rapped on the door.

Fragrant steam rose from the bath, hazing her skin, warming it to a delectable rose pink. His gaze dropped to the neckline of the unbuttoned shirt she clasped closed in one hand, then to her silky, loose trousers. She looked ripe and delicious. His hands twitched as he stepped into the bathroom.

'Tariq.'

The husky way she breathed his name recalled nights of carnal delight. He reached for her, the lingering tightness in his chest disintegrating as he wrapped his hand around her waist and felt her, warm and alluring, beneath his palm.

'I want you,' he growled, spreading his feet wide and hauling her in between his thighs. 'Now.'

Her lips tasted like heaven. Her body arched into his as he slid his hands down the sweep of her back and anchored them on her taut buttocks.

She sighed into his mouth and Tariq wanted nothing more than this, to be here with Samira.

'The bath!' She leaned back in his hold, twisting to look over her shoulder.

Tariq feasted on his view of bountiful breasts, plump above her creamy lace bra. He swallowed a groan.

Fortunately for his sanity Samira had yet to realise how utterly compelling he found her body. She didn't play coy games but always gave herself generously, participating equally in every erotic adventure.

He'd lifted his hand to caress her breast when she pulled away, bending to turn off the taps.

A tight smile curved Tariq's mouth as he appreciated the view. From her casually upswept hair, to the swell of her hips and neatly rounded bottom, Samira was all woman.

All his.

She turned, surveying him from under the long fringe of her lashes. He felt that look right to the soles of his feet.

In a more reflective moment he might worry about her ability to reduce him to molten hunger. Right now he was too busy enjoying himself.

He stepped forward, then halted, puzzled by her expression. She looked… He couldn't pin down her expression but sensed secret satisfaction. Her smile was pure Mona Lisa.

'Samira, what is it?'

She opened her eyes wide as if surprised he'd sensed the energy radiating from her. Tariq wondered that he hadn't noticed it sooner, but he'd been absorbed responding to other needs. Now he paused, surveying her face.

Her eyes glittered like faceted gems. He'd never seen them so bright. And there was something wistful about her smile that drew him on a level that had nothing to do with sex.

She was simply the most beautiful woman he'd ever seen.

His eyes traced the gentle curve of her mouth, the throb of her pulse at the base of her neck, and something punched hard and low in his belly. Something more than desire or possessiveness. Something he'd never known before.

'Samira, talk to me.'

'I have some news.' Her gaze cut from his and he noticed her hands twisting together.

Instantly Tariq tensed. He stepped forward and took her hands. They trembled in his and he frowned. 'Bad news?'

She shook her head, loose tendrils of ebony silk swirling around her throat. 'Good news. Unbelievable news.'

Her eyes met his again and heat scudded down his spine to flare out into his belly. Her radiant smile pulled his own lips wide. Anything that made her happy was worth celebrating.

'Don't keep me in suspense.'

Her hands turned in his, fingers clasping tight.

'The most wonderful news in the world. We're going to have a baby.'

CHAPTER TEN

THROUGH A HAZE of elation Samira watched Tariq's broad brow furrow in amazement. She nodded eagerly, urging him to accept it was true, though she found it hard to believe herself.

Time stood still on this moment of pure joy. The seconds slowed as he stared down at her, his features setting into lines of disbelief.

'It's true. Really.' She felt like a giddy kid, excitement fizzing in her veins.

'You told me you couldn't have children.' Tariq's eyebrows arrowed down in a black line and his tone sounded almost accusing.

'I did. That's what I thought, what I've believed for years.'

'You didn't think to check?'

Samira started at his harsh tone. This wasn't the reaction she'd expected. 'You don't sound happy.'

He shook his head as if to clear it, his expression surprisingly grim. 'I sound like a man whose wife assured him children were an impossibility.'

She frowned. Surely she imagined his disapproval? 'I was told by my specialist I couldn't have children.'

Even now those words rang like a death knell, making her shiver. For they *had* been a death knell. He'd broken the news after she'd lost her precious child. It had been a double blow, to miscarry then learn there could be no other babies in future.

'Here. You need to sit.' Tariq took her by the elbow and led her to the seat beside the bath.

Immediately she felt better. For an inexplicable moment she'd worried he wasn't pleased with her news. Samira sighed as she sat, her legs none too steady.

'Thank you. It's still a bit of a shock.'

'But you're absolutely sure?' His look was intent.

'The doctor just confirmed it.' Not just any doctor, but the best obstetrician in the capital. She slipped her hand across her abdomen, reassuring herself. 'He was just here. He assured me the earlier diagnosis was flawed. Obviously, since there's a baby.' She found her lips curving once more in a smile.

Tariq nodded. 'I thought I recognised him in the distance.'

For a moment Samira wondered how Tariq knew him, till she realised the same doctor might have attended Jasmin. She blinked and looked quickly away.

In her excitement Samira hadn't considered how her news would dredge up bittersweet memories for Tariq. No wonder he seemed a little...aloof. She'd been so wrapped up in excitement she hadn't thought of anything else.

'Doesn't he need to do further tests?'

Samira dragged her eyes back to Tariq, wary at his lack of animation. Surely, when he had time to acclimatise...?

'Yes, to make sure everything is normal. But the doctor was very reassuring and there's no question I'm pregnant.' She paused, savouring the words. They were an incantation of hope and joy. Her—a mother! 'The doctor thinks I'm already well along.'

'How is that possible?' Tariq's words sounded brusque. But then, he was still processing the news. No doubt he'd be beaming when it sank in.

'I didn't have any symptoms, except now I've started to

put on weight. Not even any morning sickness.' He didn't say anything and she felt heat climb her cheeks.

Still Tariq didn't say more, just stood watching her, his stance rigid. He was within touching distance but he hadn't reached for her since he'd helped her sit.

Suddenly that tiny distance between them seemed telling.

He'd had time now to absorb her news. Wasn't a father-to-be supposed to be pleased as well as surprised?

Tariq loved children. He was a family man through and through. Yet he watched her as if looking at a stranger.

Icy fingers played a fugue down Samira's spine. Her smile frayed around the edges.

'I realise it will mean some adjustments for Adil and Risay, to have a little brother or sister. But they're young enough to adapt.' Was that what bothered him? 'I already love them both and I promise they'll never be second best in my eyes.'

'The more the merrier?' Tariq's shoulders rose as he dredged up a deep breath. 'You were always up-front about your desire for children. Of course you're thrilled.'

'And you're not?' Looking up as he towered over her was giving her a crick in the neck. She stood up, hauling the edges of her shirt close together with stiff fingers.

'You have to admit it's…unexpected. You told me you couldn't have children.'

He'd said that before. She blinked as her skin crawled. Something wasn't right. Did he think she'd lied to him about being unable to conceive? Surely not.

Tariq looked down at those soft sherry eyes and saw hurt shimmer there. He hefted in another deep breath. He had to get hold of himself.

But from the moment Samira had said the word 'baby'

he'd frozen inside. The world had decelerated into slow motion, a sense of unreality filling him.

He'd believed he'd never have to face this again. He swallowed, a bitter taint on his tongue. For an instant he'd almost been tempted to think Samira had tricked him into fatherhood, pretending to be infertile. Till his brain had switched on. This was *Samira*. Honest, up-front Samira. She'd never behave so dishonestly.

Tariq reached out and stroked the hair off Samira's flushed cheek and she turned her head into his touch, sighing. With relief? He knew he hadn't responded as she'd hoped.

'It's very exciting news,' he managed at last. 'The twins will be delighted to have another playmate too, I'm sure.'

'You think so?' Samira smiled, her eyes sparkling. She was lit from within, almost incandescent. Tariq shied from the memory of Jasmin with that same expectant glow. And the unavoidable recollection of her months later, parchment-white and still, so very still, beneath the neatly folded hospital sheet.

'It's a miracle and a little scary.' Her hand reached out to grasp his. That was when he noticed she was trembling.

Instantly Tariq pulled her close, wrapping his arm around her slender shoulders. She leaned into him, hugging tight. How could he not have realised she'd be nervous as well as excited?

'Miracles can be a little frightening.' Tariq injected a smile into his voice. 'But you'll be in the best of hands, I promise.' Ruthlessly he thrust aside the knowledge that the best hands hadn't saved Jasmin. Samira didn't need to hear that.

'Thank you, Tariq. I know you'll look after me.' Her breath shuddered against his chest. She felt so fragile in his arms, so vulnerable. Reassuringly he tightened his hold, pretending to a certainty he was far from feeling. 'It's just…'

'Just what?'

It took her a long time to reply. When she finally did, the words came in a rush. 'I had a miscarriage four years ago.'

Her words stopped his voice. They all but stopped his heart.

He stepped back a fraction so he could look down into her face. The pain he saw there stabbed through him, slicing a furrow through his heart. She'd been pregnant?

His hands closed convulsively around her and he pulled her close, rocking her against him.

'That must have been devastating.'

'It *was*,' Samira whispered. 'It happened just after the news broke about Jackson's infidelities, when I returned to Jazeer to escape the paparazzi.'

Tariq felt her tremble and comforted her as best he could with long, slow sweeps of his hand at her back. All the time he felt a roiling burst of emotions deep in his gut. Frustration, anger and regret. Samira had gone through so much. Her lover's betrayal, public humiliation as the scandal hit the press and the paparazzi hounded her and, on top of that, such personal heartbreak.

'I had no idea. No wonder Asim kept you close in the palace.' If he'd known he'd have offered his help. But what could he have done?

'I sort of went into a meltdown.' Samira burrowed deeper into his chest. 'I didn't trust myself in the public eye and I hid out in the palace, not wanting to see anyone. I stayed there for months.'

'I'm not surprised.'

'Really?' Over-bright eyes lifted to meet his.

It felt as if he'd swallowed splinters of shattered glass when he saw the hurt in those huge eyes.

'Really.' Had she thought herself weak for taking time

to recover from such devastating blows? 'I can't imagine how you coped.' The idea of losing Risay or Adil made him break out in a cold sweat.

'I had no choice.'

Pain hammered him when he thought of her going through that alone. Tariq had known Samira for years and understood that, despite Asim's willingness to support her, Samira would have drawn in on herself, closing out the world and suffering in silence. He'd seen it when she was a kid. She didn't share her hurt. That was one of the reasons her proposal in Paris had blindsided him, because she'd opened up enough to let him glimpse her pain at not being able to conceive.

'You're not alone now,' he found himself saying. 'This is our baby and I'll be here to take care of you.'

He must have said the right thing because Samira's face lit up with a glow that rivalled the luminous desert sunset.

'Thank you, Tariq. I needed to hear that.'

He took her hand in his, so small yet so capable, and raised it to his lips. She tasted of sweet, heady woman and despite the gravity of the moment Tariq registered his body's eager response.

He'd never wanted a woman the way he wanted Samira. The thought of her, sexy and ripe with his child, sent his hormones into overdrive.

Until his brain engaged again.

She'd had a miscarriage. She'd been told she'd never be able to conceive again, yet against the odds she had. It didn't take a genius to realise the risks for Samira and the child had to be higher than average.

He mustn't do anything to endanger them. She might be in her second trimester, when the risk of miscarriage was supposed to lessen, but Tariq knew how unpredictable, how downright dangerous, pregnancy could be.

The image of Jasmin's still face rose again. She'd died

giving birth to the babies he'd planted within her, the babies he'd married her to acquire.

Tariq shuddered, fear icing his spine. He wouldn't let history repeat itself. He'd take every possible precaution.

And, he vowed, he'd do it without adding to Samira's natural anxiety. After one miscarriage she must be nervous about the outcome of this pregnancy. She didn't need his fears compounding her own.

'Come on,' he urged, gently brushing Samira's shirt from her shoulders, valiantly ignoring the delicious bounty of full breasts in that made-for-seduction lace bra. 'Let's get you into that bath while it's still warm.'

Samira complied with an alacrity that had him almost bursting out of his too-tight skin. She shimmied out of her trousers, wriggling her hips in a tantalising display that made him swallow hard. Tariq had to turn away, pretending to adjust the water temperature when she undid her bra and her ripe breasts swung free. His palms itched to reach for them and his groin tightened unbearably.

The final straw came as she shoved her panties off and swiped her hand over her waist and the slight swell of her belly. Her beatific smile stole his breath but the sight of her naked body, indescribably lush and feminine, almost broke him.

Quickly Tariq reached for her arm, ignoring the sultry invitation in her eyes.

'Hold onto me as you step in. Don't slip.'

'Of course I won't slip. You've got me.' Her words were a breathy laugh of joy that curled around his heart, making it beat fast and hard.

Stoically Tariq averted his eyes from the sight of her rose-tipped breasts bobbing in the water, the shadow between slender thighs that parted as he watched. Heat speared him.

'Join me?' Her voice was a throaty invitation, her fingers clinging to his. She knew as well as he did that he'd never once refused an invitation to get naked with her. On the contrary, he'd shocked her once or twice with the ways and places he'd chosen to sate the ever-present carnal desire they shared.

Tariq forced himself to stand tall, pulling his hand from hers. Samira's smile vanished, her brow wrinkling.

'Relax now.' He couldn't help himself and bent down to kiss her cheek, inhaling her sweetness. 'It's been a big day.'

Finally she nodded, disappointment tinging her expression. 'Yes. It's been a lot to take in.'

Tariq made himself step back. 'Your maid will be waiting in the bedroom when you're ready to get out. Just call and let her help you. Yes?' He waited till she agreed, then turned and made himself walk, stiff-legged, out of the bathroom.

He ached all over. He wasn't used to denying himself the pleasure of Samira's body. He'd never known such temptation as watching her strip before him, knowing she carried his child.

He'd found pleasure with Jasmin. He'd been thrilled by her pregnancy. But he'd never experienced anything like this.

Tariq wiped his hand across his face and discovered he was sweating.

Samira was pregnant with his child.

He would do whatever it took to keep the pair of them safe. He would take no chances. Tariq closed his eyes, feeling deep in his gut that churning fear of failure he'd known only once before.

His imagination failed him at the idea of losing her as he'd lost Jasmin.

No! He wouldn't let it happen again.

Not to Samira.

* * *

'Are you sure there's nothing bothering you, Samira?' Over the long-distance connection her sister-in-law, Jacqui, sounded concerned.

'No, no. I'm fine.'

'Except?'

Samira heard Jacqui's determination to get to the bottom of things. It was a trait that had made her a successful journalist before she'd taken to writing books.

'Come on, you can talk to me. Something's not right.'

Samira sighed and sat back in her favourite comfy chair, the one Tariq had transported all the way from Jazeer to her work room. Staring at the mountains bathed in shades of pink and gold by the dying sun, she reminded herself how lucky she was. The doctor had allayed the worst of her fears, assuring her there was no reason she shouldn't carry this baby to term.

'Everything is fine, truly. I don't have any complaints.' She paused, hearing Jacqui's waiting silence. 'It's just that Tariq is...' Again she hesitated. How could she admit her husband hadn't been in her bed in the weeks since she'd broken the news about the baby? Or that she missed him so badly his absence marred her joy at this miracle pregnancy?

How far she'd come from the woman who'd blithely assumed she could have a paper marriage with Tariq. Once she'd experienced his love-making she'd been hooked. Yet it wasn't just sex she missed, it was the intimacy. The pillow talk, the tenderness, the feeling of wellbeing and closeness that had no equal in her experience.

Was it anxiety about the pregnancy that made her so needy?

A huff of laughter came over the phone. 'If you ask me Tariq is just like Asim—proud, assertive and overprotective. It's a wonder to me that two such strong, opinionated men grew to be such good friends.'

'They bonded when they were very young. You know our home life wasn't easy.' Now, that was an understatement! 'And, from what Asim said, Tariq's upbringing was tough. His uncle expected him to be a man from an early age. I don't think there was time for fun, except when he visited us. He was too busy preparing for the demands of the sheikhdom.'

'From what Asim said? Hasn't Tariq told you about his past?'

Samira shrugged. 'I've known him all my life, so I know the important things.' Yet he'd surprised her. He was more complex, powerful and determined than she'd thought. 'Tariq isn't the sort of man to open up, seeking sympathy.'

'That makes two of you.' She paused. 'Maybe that's the problem. Perhaps you need to open up more to each other.'

Samira opened her mouth to protest, then stopped. 'Is that what you and Asim did?'

Again that gentle huff of laughter. 'Getting your brother to talk about feelings was almost impossible.'

'You managed it.' Asim and Jacqui were blissfully happy. They were one of the reasons she'd had the nerve to propose marriage. She'd wanted at least a modified version of their happy family, even if it was centred around respect and child-rearing rather than passionate devotion. She drew a fortifying breath. 'How did you do it?'

'What? Drag your brother, kicking and screaming, out of his comfort zone to confront his feelings?' Jacqui paused and Samira sat forward, eager for the answer. 'It wasn't easy.' There was no laugh in her voice now. 'I shared myself with him. I was totally honest.'

Samira cringed. Tariq already he knew her secrets: her desire for a family and her miscarriage, her hopes for this child. Surely that was enough? All she wanted was to resume the intimacy they'd shared until last month.

'Samira? Are you there?'

'Yes.'

'But you're not sure you wanted to hear that?'

Jacqui was too perceptive. 'You've given me a lot to think about.'

She just wasn't sure it was the answer for her.

Samira smoothed the rich cream satin over her thighs. It felt decadently luxurious. A baby bulge didn't stop a woman from appreciating beautiful lingerie.

She twisted in front of the workshop's full-length mirror. The neckline plunged deep, edged with the exquisite embroidery she'd commissioned in the mountains. She'd placed an order for more, knowing the delicate finery on the translucent fabric was just right for this design.

She had long-term plans to launch an exclusive range of lingerie. The project gave her a new creative outlet and would provide valuable income for the village women.

Her mouth twisted. Who'd have thought pregnancy would inspire her to design slinky nightgowns? She might be halfway through her pregnancy but hormones only made her more aware of her body's needs.

Or maybe that was Tariq.

Her hands bunched in the slithery fabric, her pulse tripping. Her husband made her hot and bothered with just a look or the casual brush of his hand.

Which was tragic when a casual brush of the hand was all she'd had from him since she'd told him about the baby. That and his solicitous grip at her elbow whenever she descended the long staircase to the royal reception rooms. He always managed to be at her side then, the epitome of protectiveness.

As if she were some feeble, ancient relative. The thought infuriated her. And hurt.

A commotion at the door had her spinning around just as a tiny body launched itself at her.

'Mama!' Small arms wrapped around her legs, hugging tight.

'Risay.' She bent to pick him up but wasn't fast enough.

'Let me.' Tariq was already there, disengaging hands that she saw now were sticky with honey, and lifting Risay high. 'I'm sorry about your...' He stopped as he took in her décolletage.

Instantly her nipples tightened, grazing the soft fabric. She drew in a sharp breath as heat shafted through her body at his look.

Naked but for a thin layer of satin, she felt too exposed. The speculative gleam in Tariq's eyes told her he hadn't missed her response. Worse, it created a needy, melting sensation between her legs.

'Mama!' Risay leaned towards her, arms outstretched, and she dragged her attention back to him, smiling at his cheeky grin.

'He's not supposed to bother you while you're working.' Tariq's voice was like the stroke of silken gauze across her bare arms and shoulders. She shivered and kept her eyes on Risay.

'I don't mind.' She took Risay's hand and leaned in, brushing his cheek with a gentle kiss. 'It's rare that they escape Sofia's eagle eye.' Footsteps made her turn. Sure enough, there was Sofia, tutting under her breath.

'My apologies, sir, ma'am.' She turned to the toddler who gave her a broad grin. 'And as for you, Master Trouble, you'll come back right now and finish your meal.'

'Mama,' he said defiantly.

Samira couldn't prevent a tiny smile of delight. Discipline was important, of course, and her hours in the work room were precious if she wanted to keep her business ticking over till she was ready to devote more time to it again. But she couldn't be angry that Risay wanted to be with her. Or that he called her Mama.

'I'll be along soon. After you've finished eating.'

Finally, with pouts that failed to hide his triumph, Risay let Sofia carry him out.

Tariq made to follow till Samira put out her hand. She'd avoided taking Jacqui's advice for too long. Now she was desperate enough to try even that.

'Don't go.' Slowly he turned and her breath stalled as she met his eyes. Her skin tightened, the hairs lifting on her arms at the intensity of that stare. Her hand dropped to her side as she battled that familiar upsurge of longing.

'Please?'

CHAPTER ELEVEN

TARIQ COULDN'T TAKE his eyes off Samira. The sheen of the clingy material she wore complemented the glow of her skin and the luminous brightness of her sherry-gold eyes. Stoically he tried not to stare at the swell of her breasts, tip-tilted with hard little nubs that thrust so invitingly towards him. The delicious sweep from waist to hip. The pronounced curve of her belly where she cradled his child.

He swallowed and ripped his gaze back up again.

His wife. His for the taking.

He read the invitation in her eyes and had to weld his feet to the floor rather than stalk back and haul her into his arms.

How he wanted her.

How he'd missed her.

All these weeks it had been hell holding back: being at her side in public or with the boys. Making sure she didn't work herself too hard. And all the time keeping his hands to himself.

When he did allow himself to touch her it was exquisite torture. He wanted so much more than her arm in his, the inadvertent brush of her hip or breast as they stood together, presiding at some function.

'Yes?' The word was harsh as gravel. He cleared his throat and tried for a softer tone. 'You wanted something?'

There was a flash in Samira's eyes that might have been anger but it was gone before he could be sure.

'Won't you stay for a while? I rarely see you.'

He saw her daily. Yet he knew what she meant. He'd been careful not to be alone with her.

'My schedule's very busy.' Nevertheless he moved back into the room and saw some of the tension ease from her slim shoulders.

'Surely you have some time for me?'

Some time! *All* his time was devoted to the complex issue of Samira and how she fitted in his life. How best to look after her and their child.

'Is there something wrong?' Tariq noticed the tiny smudges under her eyes. He frowned. He was used to her blooming with good health. Even now she looked radiant, but those shadows told a different story.

He crossed the room and took her arm, registering the softness of her inner arm and the swish of shimmery material against her naked skin as he led her to an armchair.

'Tell me about it.' He waited till she took a seat before retreating to lean against her work table. But her subtle cinnamon scent wafted across his senses. It was more intoxicating than any manufactured perfume.

'You've been avoiding me,' she said at last.

Tariq shrugged. 'My diary is full with the multilateral negotiations and the rebuilding project on top of all the usual commitments.'

Samira angled her head as if to view him better. He folded his arms.

'You know what I mean.' Her voice dropped to a low, sultry note. 'You don't come to my bed any more.'

Now she *had* surprised him. He hadn't expected a direct confrontation.

Why? Because she's so shy and docile? An inner voice sneered at his foolishness. Of course Samira would take the bull by the horns. For all her subtlety and grace in dealing with the public and fractious VIPs, she was no pushover.

She could be surprisingly forthright. The fact she'd had the nerve to propose marriage to him proved that.

And yet… Tariq sensed it took a lot for her to confront him. Her hands twisted in her lap while her neck and shoulders screamed tension.

'You want sex?' His mind raced, calculating how long it would take to get her out of that slinky bit of nothing and flat on her back beneath him.

It took far too much effort to crush the urge to act.

Tariq knew his duty. His uncle had drummed a sense of responsibility into him by the time he could walk, preparing for the day he'd be ruler.

Samira had a history of miscarriage. His duty was to keep her and their child safe. If that meant staying out of her bed for a few months, he'd do it. He'd do everything to protect her. Just as he had the country's top specialist on call and had cut back the hours of evening functions so Samira could rest.

He'd take no chances.

A shadow flickered in his soul and a chill crept up his backbone, lifting the hairs on his nape one by one. He drew a slow breath, not quite managing to dispel the fear he'd fail Samira as he'd failed Jasmin.

'Yes.' Samira shook her head, her brow furrowing. 'No. Not just sex.'

Tariq waited. Her shoulders lifted and dropped and he swallowed hard as those lush breasts jiggled temptingly.

'I want…' She shook her head and again he caught the perfume of her skin.

Everything about his wife—from her voice, the perfume of her skin, the taste of her on his tongue, to the lush perfection of her body—made him want more. Made him want in ways too numerous to calculate.

Tariq's hands clenched on the edge of the worktop. 'You want…?'

'I don't think I can put it into words.'

Despite his certainty that it would be better for them both if he found an excuse to leave, he didn't shift. How could he look after her if he didn't understand her?

'Try me.'

Samira looked up at him watching her, the intensity of his gaze wrapping around her, making warmth curl within. Yet he gave nothing away.

She'd come this far. All she had to do was be honest. *Share yourself*, Jacqui had said.

Unfortunately Samira had little experience of that. She'd learned to keep herself to herself in the ways that really mattered. But if it was worth having it was worth fighting for. Tariq, and the precious sense of wellbeing he'd given her before, were worth having.

'You know Asim and I weren't close to our parents?'

Tariq's eyebrows slanted in surprise at the change of subject. 'I knew.'

'You've heard their marriage wasn't easy?' Asim wouldn't have discussed it and Tariq wouldn't have asked, but he'd have to have been deaf not to hear the whispers.

'I don't listen to rumour. I prefer to deal in facts.'

Samira compressed her lips. Was he being deliberately unhelpful or just chivalrous?

'They lived in a world of their own. When all was well I never saw them because they were wrapped up in each other. But more often it was a war zone. Screaming rows and doors slamming, glass smashing and angry tirades.' She brushed her hands over the shivering skin of her arms. 'They were jealous and suspected other lovers. The best times were when they were away and we were alone with the staff.'

'I'm sorry. That must have been hard.'

Samira hesitated, groping for words. 'I'm not telling

you this to get sympathy, but so you understand what it was like.'

'I understand.'

But did he?

'The thing is…' She looked down to see she'd bunched the rich satin into a taut knot. Instantly she opened her hands and smoothed out the crushed fabric. 'The thing is, they didn't just play out their dramas between them. They used us.'

Samira kept her eyes down, not wanting to read Tariq's expression as acid memories made her flesh crawl.

'Each used to interrogate me, trying to use me as a spy against the other. I found out years later that a diplomat was dismissed because I told my father how he smiled and laughed when he was with my mother. I thought it nice *someone* laughed in the palace but my father was convinced they were having an affair. Possibly because he was having one with my nanny at the time.'

'You shouldn't have had to go through that.' The rumble of Tariq's voice drew her head up. His expression was sombre.

'It could have been worse.' She paused. 'It took me a long time to learn to be cautious but I learned my lesson when I was thirteen.' Samira stopped and focused on trying to slow her too-fast pulse.

'My mother invited me to tea with a friend and I was so excited to be included I didn't realise what was happening till too late. Her "friend" turned out to be a journalist, pumping me for information about my father. She took innocent anecdotes and twisted them into the worst kind of slimy innuendo about my father. The more I tried to set the story straight, the worse it got, with my mother putting words in my mouth and it all going down on record.'

Samira sank back in her seat, hating that it had been her mother of all people who'd made her feel unclean.

'My father managed to quash the story but my parents separated. Publicly the story was they were busy with regal responsibilities in different places.'

She met Tariq's grim stare and shrugged. 'I blamed myself but I finally learned to keep myself to myself.'

It was a lesson she'd stuck to until she'd met Jackson Brent and, in the throes of romantic excitement, thrown caution to the wind. His betrayal had cured her of romance and almost stolen her ability to trust.

Yet she trusted Tariq.

He'd moved away from the table to stand before her. The expression in his eyes made her heart somersault with hope.

Jacqui had been right. She just needed to open up to her husband. Explain and clear up whatever was holding him back. Then they could regain the easy, satisfying relationship she'd so enjoyed. Relief filled her. The unpalatable task of talking about the past would be worth it.

'You can't blame yourself for their marriage failing.'

'Eventually I worked that out. Plus I realised I didn't want a marriage like theirs.'

Her gaze lingered on the impressive breadth of Tariq's shoulders and chest and she congratulated herself on having made a far better marriage. She hadn't trusted so-called love. She'd married a man she respected, a man of integrity.

Yet being so close to him sent her wayward hormones into a chaos of yearning excitement.

'I told you this so you'd understand how much our marriage means to me.' She smiled up at him. 'After my parents' destructive marriage and my failed relationship, it took a lot even to consider marriage. I don't trust easily. But you've made this...' Samira waved her hand wide, suddenly on an emotional brink at the thought of all Tariq had done for her.

He'd given her so much. Not only had he shared his boys, he'd created a place for her in his world, accepting her and caring for her. She felt safe, content, part of the sort of family she'd never thought she'd have, yet with the freedom to pursue her dreams.

And then there was the child she carried.

She put her hands on the arms of her chair, ready to lever herself up.

'Don't! There's no need to get up.' Tariq dragged a straight-backed chair from the table and sat down, facing her, his long legs folded back beneath the seat. 'So, you're happy here. That's excellent.'

Samira blinked. 'More than that. What we've shared— it's more than I'd believed possible.' Despite her confident proposal, she'd wondered how well two virtual strangers could live and work together.

'You've been wonderful, Tariq. Thoughtful and generous, and reassuring when I need it.' It was as if he sensed and responded to her fears for the baby.

'It's my pleasure to look after you.' His words were crisply formal, as if she hadn't got through to him at all.

'I'm not talking about being looked after.' Her brow pleated as she sought the right words. 'What you've given me is precious and I want you to know I appreciate it.' She smiled, rubbing at her baby bulge as she felt the fluttery movements of their child.

Tariq followed her gesture and stiffened. Samira was thrilled he'd given her a child. No surprises there. That was why she'd married him, to become a mother.

He exhaled slowly. No man liked to feel used but Samira came perilously close to making him feel that now.

He hadn't been consulted about this child. If he had, he'd have admitted the twins were enough for him. After losing Jasmin in labour, another child was the last thing on his mind.

His blood chilled thinking about that time.

What did Samira want from him? Why tell him now about her miserable childhood? He felt frustrated and appalled by it but could do nothing to alter the past.

Despite his considerable experience, women could still be a mystery.

He watched Samira closely, noting her over-bright eyes and flushed cheeks. She was emotional, he'd almost say overwrought, except there was no question that she was happy.

'Thank you,' he murmured. 'I'm pleased you're content.' Samira had been fulsome in her thanks and, despite the demons that rode him, he understood how precious this baby was to her. 'I want you to be happy.'

She nodded, her eyes glowing, and Tariq stood abruptly. He needed to leave before he did something unforgivable, like maul the woman he'd pledged not to touch.

He'd done his research. He knew sex with Samira wasn't likely to endanger her or the baby. But how likely had it been that Jasmin, after a completely normal, healthy pregnancy, should die? He couldn't take the risk. Not again. Not Samira.

'I need to leave, but I'll see you later with the boys.'

'Wait!' Samira stood too, her hand smoothing the nightgown over her bump. 'You're going? But you haven't answered me.'

'There was no question.' Heat seared him with each passing second. He had to get out of here before his resolve cracked.

She drew herself up. Yet even when she looked downright regal all he could think of was how good she'd feel in his arms, melting against him. How good she'd taste.

'I want to sleep with you.' Her words were pure, husky

temptation to a man on the edge of control. 'But I want more too. More of *us*. The way we were before I told you about the baby.' Her eyes held a dewy sheen of happiness he'd thought reserved for their child. But now Samira was looking at him in a way that did strange things to his internal organs. He couldn't identify the sensation and that disturbed him.

'Being with you...' Her shoulders lifted as she spread her arms palm upwards. 'I can't tell you how much our marriage means. It's changed me. I never expected I'd feel anything like this.'

Tariq stiffened.

She hadn't expected to feel anything like this?

Like what?

He remembered Jasmin's soft, hopeful gaze whenever he'd entered a room, whenever they were together. They'd contracted to marry but somewhere during their dynastic marriage she'd fallen in love.

And he'd been unable to return that love. He'd felt her disappointment in every searching, loving look.

Tariq swallowed hard, tasting the rusty metal tang of horror as he registered the softening in Samira's expression.

'I want to be a wife to you in every way, Tariq.' Her smile could light up a city. But it could devastate too. His chest cracked wide as he saw what was in her eyes.

Love.

Love for him.

A love he was congenitally incapable of returning.

His breath caught, snared by his galloping heartbeat. Sweat broke out across his forehead and there was a drumming in his ears as past and present merged. Pressure built in his chest as if from welling emotions. Except he didn't do emotion, not of that sort.

This couldn't be happening again. A wife who looked

to him for love. A wife carrying his child. A wife who yearned for something that wasn't in him to give. A wife he feared he couldn't keep safe from hurt.

The day Jasmin had died the doctor had looked at him with sympathy, believing he dealt with a heartbroken husband. Tariq had felt like a sham, utterly unworthy.

Tariq had assured himself theirs was a decent marriage, a practical one, that he'd been a thoughtful and loyal husband even as he'd regretted Jasmin's unfortunate *tendre*. But it was only when she'd died that the enormity of what he'd done had smashed into him, blasting away cosy excuses. Jasmin had lost her life because of him and his need for heirs.

Now the past reinvented itself. He saw it in Samira's hopeful expression. In her outstretched hand.

Tariq's heart slammed against his ribs, his skin breaking into a clammy sweat as the walls pushed in on him, the weight of them crushing the air from his lungs.

He stepped back and watched her arm fall. His gut went into freefall as he saw surprise morph into hurt. But he couldn't lie. Not even for her. 'I'm sorry, Samira, but you're asking too much.'

Tariq spun on his heel and strode from the room.

CHAPTER TWELVE

YOU'RE ASKING TOO MUCH.

The words had hung in the air between them too long. It had been weeks since Tariq had burst out with them and still they bit deep, hurting just as keenly as the day he'd said them.

Samira looked down the long table lit by antique candelabras. Beyond the twenty guests invited to this intimate royal dinner sat Tariq, resplendent in white robes and a head scarf edged with gold.

He faced her down the table but his attention was on his guests. He conversed with the American ambassador and some leading entrepreneurs while at the same time making a couple of visiting provincial leaders feel welcome.

Tariq handled his responsibilities easily. He was an expert negotiator. According to his staff he was a born administrator. His people loved him because he was a man of action who ruled fairly and provided well for them.

The twins adored him. He made time for them in ways her father never had. And, if Tariq was a fraction too strict on discipline, she and Sofia moderated his demands.

Few men could handle so many responsibilities. Yet Tariq did. Nothing was too much effort.

Except being with his wife.

That was *asking too much.*

Bile filled Samira's mouth and she choked it back, her

knife and fork clattering to her plate. The delicious meal turned to ashes in her mouth.

Tariq made time for everyone but her.

As if sensing her regard, he looked up.

Even from this distance his laser-bright stare captured her, pinning her to the seat. Samira's heartbeat fluttered, her breath quickening. Despite the heavy weight of pregnancy she felt that telltale softening at her core in preparation for his touch.

A touch that would never come.

Samira bit her lower lip before it could tremble.

She despised her weakness for a man who patently didn't want her.

Oh, he'd been happy enough to take her when they were first married. He'd *insisted* on it, as if a platonic marriage was an affront to his manhood.

But once her waistline had thickened, and she'd become more apple than hourglass, Tariq had lost interest. Her appeal had clearly been skin-deep.

She'd known her looks would fade with age but hadn't expected to lose her allure so soon, or realised how devastating that would be.

Samira choked down aching self-pity and forced her gaze to the blur of faces around the table.

Tariq had made it abundantly clear she was in the same category as the multitude of women who'd kept him company before and after his first marriage. They'd been gorgeous and expendable. Once he'd had his fill, they'd been history.

Was there even now some beauty waiting for this dinner to end so he'd come to her? Pain knifed Samira's ribs, slashing at her, tearing her breath.

After all, she'd given him permission to take lovers. She didn't want to believe it, not after what they'd shared, but, having experienced Tariq's phenomenal sex drive, she doubted he'd stay celibate long.

Nothing could have reinforced the fact she was a poor second to his beloved first wife more than the way he avoided her. He treated her charmingly, always concerned for her wellbeing, but in an avuncular way, as if she was a charge to be cared for, not a wife to be cherished.

How dared he?

Fury was a pummelling beat high in her chest.

He'd seduced her for his pleasure, then left her high and dry when his interest waned. As if she could be dismissed once he'd had his fill!

How was she supposed to continue in this marriage? Better never to have given in to his seduction and lived as strangers than succumb to his charisma, fall for the man, then have him reject her.

Pain jabbed deep as realisation struck.

Fall for the man...

Samira sucked in a panicked breath. No, it wasn't that. It couldn't be. She'd never be foolish enough to risk her heart again by falling in love with any man. Not even Mr Almost Perfect Tariq.

Yet her anguished heart somersaulted at the very thought of the word.

Love.

Love for Tariq.

Had she fooled herself all this time, telling herself she could have everything she wanted with him but not risk her heart?

'Your Highness, are you all right?' The words reached her through a thick fog. 'Your Highness?'

Slowly she dragged her head around to find Nicolas Roussel leaning close, his hair gleaming gold in the wavering darkness that edged her vision.

'Do you need a doctor?' The Frenchman's voice was

low and urgent. He reached as if to touch her arm, then hesitated, as if remembering her royal status. His blue eyes were concerned.

At least there was one man here who cared about her!

Even as the thought lodged, Samira knew she was being melodramatic. Tariq cared. Just not enough.

The thought brought a sob to her lips and she clapped a hand over her mouth, horrified that her emotions had her teetering on the brink.

Tariq had enjoyed her as a lover till her sexual allure faded, and he cared about her as the stand-in mother for the twins, as his consort and hostess. He just didn't care about her the way she did him.

Love.

Samira's heart pounded so hard it felt like it might jump out of her chest.

How long had she been pretending to herself?

How long since she'd fallen for her husband?

'I'm calling a doctor.' A chair scraped as Nicolas made to stand.

'No!' Her hand shot out and grabbed his wrist. As if from a distance she saw her fingers wrap, white-knuckled, around his arm. She couldn't seem to let go. 'I'm all right, truly.'

Samira tried for a smile and knew she'd failed when he looked at her doubtfully.

'Truly.' She tried again, her tense facial muscles stretching. 'It's just...' she leaned towards him and he bent close '...sometimes I get a little uncomfortable.'

His gaze skated across her belly, then up again.

Samira nodded, prising her fingers loose from his arm and sitting back in her seat, willing herself to look calm despite her too-rapid pulse and the sick lurching of her stomach. It was a half-truth, after all, since she'd suffered from indigestion recently. Better to let her guest think it was that bothering her than the discovery she was in love with her husband. A husband who had rejected her.

Pain wrapped gnarled hands around her heart, squeezing tight.

'I understand.' Nicholas's smile was warm. 'My sister recently had a baby. She said sitting for too long was difficult.'

'Ah, you *do* understand.' Samira prided herself on her light tone, as if she had nothing on her mind but a little heartburn. She'd spent years learning to project grace and charm even when her private world had been a disaster. Desperately she dredged up every lesson she'd learned and gave him a dazzling smile. 'Tell me…' She leaned closer. 'Did your sister have a boy or a girl?'

The next course was being served when Samira looked up to discover Tariq staring down the table. His jaw was tight, his mouth a grim line. And the look he sent Nicolas Roussel should have incinerated the charming Frenchman where he sat.

Samira's breath stalled as hope fluttered high in her chest. Surely that incendiary stare signalled possessiveness? She'd never seen Tariq jealous, but that fixed glare held an unmistakeable threat.

Her heart took up a quick, excited rhythm.

Until Tariq's gaze shifted to her and his face went completely blank. One minute she could have sworn she saw bloodlust in his eyes, the next she was left wondering if it had been a trick of the light.

Tariq inclined his head infinitesimally, favouring her with the small, polite smile which was the most animation she ever saw in him now.

How she hated that smile. It reminded her of all they'd once shared and all she still craved.

Then he turned to the ambassador and didn't look her way again, clearly dismissing her from his thoughts.

Samira was surprised no one at her end of the table noticed the sound of her heart cracking wide open.

Tariq looked up from the draft treaty document as the
door to his private study slammed open. One look at his
wife's taut features and he surged to his feet. She was in
the final stages of pregnancy and he was constantly on
tenterhooks, wary of a crisis.

'That will be all for now,' he told his secretary, his eyes
fixed on Samira.

Never had she come to his office without invitation.
Their lives proceeded in neat, contained patterns, inter-
secting only at official functions and when they spent time
with the boys.

She looked tense. Was it the baby? Tension knotted his
gut. He started towards her, then stopped at the look she
sent him. Not pain or distress, but anger.

Tariq frowned. In all the time they'd been married he'd
never seen Samira furious. In fact he hadn't seen anger on
her features since she'd been a kid. He hadn't realised it before but even in her teens Samira had been self-contained,
as if she controlled her natural volatility.

Finally they were alone, his secretary closing the door
behind him.

'Won't you sit down?'

She lifted her chin and regarded him along her pert
nose. His breath snagged. She'd never looked more beautiful, more alluring, her eyes glittering bright as gems, her
lush body vibrating with passion. He wanted to reach out
and stroke away the tension in her shoulders, kiss her into
compliance, mould his hands to her deliciously rounded
belly and…

'You cancelled my meeting.'

Tariq blinked, trying to get his mind back into gear.

'You're not denying it?' Her hands went to her hips,

pulling the red silk of her loose dress tight, accentuating her heavily pregnant form. Could she feel his baby moving inside?

He cleared his throat and forced his gaze up, stoically ignoring the inevitable tension in his groin. Every time he looked at her he felt it. Every time he thought of her. Keeping his distance was killing him.

'You're concerned about a missed meeting?'

'I'm concerned...' she paused, dragged in a breath '...that you believe you have the right to interfere with my schedule.'

'Ah. The meeting in the mountain villages.'

She nodded. 'We were going to discuss the opportunities for local women. Yet I find it's been removed from my diary with no explanation.'

'It was to take place at the same time as the redevelopment meeting but as I'm no longer available it will be rescheduled. Besides, it's a long way to the mountains now you're so far through your pregnancy. You need to be careful of yourself.'

Given her militant look he refused to admit he'd cancelled the meeting solely to prevent her travelling late in pregnancy. He wanted Samira here, where the best medical care was available.

He thrust from his mind the fact that hadn't saved Jasmin.

Samira's delicate eyebrows arched high. 'I'm careful. Besides, I have people fussing around me if I so much as lift a finger.'

Tariq nodded. He was taking no chances with her wellbeing.

'Do you have any idea when it will be rescheduled?' Her narrowed eyes told him she wasn't convinced.

Tariq spread his hands. 'I leave those details to my staff but I doubt it will be soon.'

For a full minute Samira didn't say anything and it

struck him how much he missed the easy camaraderie they'd once shared. Being with her had been pure pleasure, not just in bed, but out of it too. Until she'd announced her pregnancy. Until he'd seen love shining in her eyes and known he couldn't give her what she wanted.

Tariq looked again. It wasn't love he read in her face.

'Very well.' She drew a slow breath. 'I'll have my secretary organise a separate meeting with the women's representatives. I have some business proposals that won't wait.' Before he could voice an objection she added, 'I'll invite them here to the capital.'

'An excellent idea.' He'd prefer it if Samira reduced the hours she spent working, but at least she'd given up her plan to travel. His breathing eased.

'I'll ask Nicolas to attend. His expertise is invaluable.'

Tariq stiffened. Was that provocation in her bright eyes as she turned and left the room? Had she guessed how he hated the sight of her with Roussel?

It didn't matter how often he reminded himself the man was capable, trustworthy and honest. The sight of Samira smiling with the Frenchman, so obviously attuned to him, set Tariq's teeth on edge.

Roussel had his wife's ear and her smiles while Tariq was forced to kick his heels at a distance. It didn't matter that he was the one who'd rebuffed Samira. Or that caution decreed he keep his distance. The strain of holding back from her drove him close to breaking point.

Roussel, of all people! Tariq hadn't missed the fact that the Frenchman had the blond hair, slim build and charming smile of Samira's first lover, Jackson Brent. Clearly she was drawn to the type.

A type that was altogether different from Tariq's towering bulk. Of course it was. She'd made no bones about the fact she'd married him for his children, not himself.

And if she'd enjoyed sex with him… Well, hadn't he made sure she did? That meant nothing.

A crash reverberated as his fist slammed into the wall. Tariq looked down, vaguely surprised at the blood scoring his knuckles. Pain wrapped round his hand and flashed up his arm.

Could he have got it wrong?

Was it possible his wife wasn't in love with him after all?

Samira gasped as pain wrapped around her and she clung to the shower screen. All day she'd felt out of sorts, unable to settle and her back aching. Now she knew why. Her baby was coming early. What had begun as ripples of discomfort had grown into full-blown contractions so fierce she had trouble remembering to breathe.

Was it supposed to be like this so quickly? She hadn't had time even to get out of the bathroom after trying to ease her discomfort with a warm shower.

Panic rose. If she slipped she doubted she could get up. She'd imagined a slow onset of labour, nothing so intense and overwhelming. What if something was wrong? What if her baby was in danger?

Suddenly the distance to the door seemed never ending.

Belatedly she remembered to slow her breathing, concentrate on exhaling. When at last the pain abated, her gaze snagged on the phone by the bath. Slowly, her hand groping for support, she made her way to it.

'Yes?' The deep voice burred in her ear as another contraction began.

Samira opened her mouth but only managed a gasp.

'Who is this?'

She clung to the receiver, her hand shaking. 'Tariq,' she finally managed. It was a hoarse whisper, the best she could manage, but he didn't answer. Her phone clattered to the floor.

Fear notched high and she blinked back tears of frustration. She needed Tariq. Here. Now. To tell her everything was okay and that the baby would be fine.

Samira rode out another contraction, bracing herself against the cool tiled wall, trying to force down fear that, despite her uneventful pregnancy, she might lose this baby too.

The door crashed open.

'Ah, *habibti*.' The deep voice curled reassuringly around her. 'It's all right. I'm here. I'll look after you.'

She closed her eyes as strong arms wrapped around her naked body and lifted her high against a solid chest.

'Tariq.' She breathed deep, inhaling that unique tang that was his, her body melting into the comfort of his embrace. 'I thought you hadn't heard me. I thought—'

'Shh. It's all right. I've got you. I won't leave your side.'

Hours later Samira looked up into eyes that had darkened to moss green. That wide, proud forehead was wrinkled with concern but his smile was brilliant.

'She looks like you,' he murmured in a voice that brushed like velvet over her skin.

'Right now I'm not sure that's a good thing.' Euphoric and still stunned at the abrupt but safe delivery of their wonderful, tiny daughter, Samira had no illusions about her appearance. She'd be exhausted if she weren't floating in seventh heaven.

'It's an excellent thing.' Tariq stepped closer, holding their child in the crook of his arm. Samira's heart rolled over at the sight of him holding that tiny, precious life so gently. 'You're the most beautiful woman I've ever known. No one can hold a candle to you.'

Samira told herself he was being kind but the way his eyes gleamed as he looked between her and the baby stopped the words in her mouth. He looked...smitten.

She blinked, fighting back what she told herself were tears of exhaustion.

'Samira? What is it?' Instantly Tariq was at her side. 'Are you in pain?' Already he was reaching for the call button to summon medical staff.

She shook her head. 'I'm just a little overcome.'

Not just by the birth, which had been unusually short for a first delivery. But by Tariq. He'd been with her the whole time, a rock to cling to, his words of encouragement just what she needed, his strength giving her strength.

Through it all she'd seen in his eyes something far more profound than concern for her physical wellbeing. No husband could have been more tender, more supportive or proud.

No matter what he'd said before, Tariq *cared*. She knew it as surely as she knew she'd just been through a life-changing experience.

Carefully he sat on the edge of the hospital bed. 'Everything will be all right.'

Looking into his glowing eyes Samira could believe it. Surely the miracle she'd hoped for had happened? He wasn't distancing himself now, erecting barriers between them.

He reached out to brush the hair back from her face, his touch a gentle caress of her flushed cheek.

Slowly, infinitely slowly, he leaned forward to press his lips to hers in the sweetest of kisses. Her lips parted and she tasted the intriguing salty, male tang of him. His tongue slicked hers, drawing her essence into his mouth, and she sighed at the rightness of it.

'Sleep now, Samira.' The words washed over her as her eyelids fluttered shut.

She smiled. Beyond all expectation everything was going to be all right.

CHAPTER THIRTEEN

SAMIRA WATCHED SILENTLY from the doorway as Tariq paced the nursery with little Layla in his arms. As ever, her heart somersaulted in her chest as she saw him with their daughter. There was no doubt she was the apple of his eye, as precious to him as the twins.

He'd always been good with children, hadn't he? It was one of the reasons Samira had married him.

Pain scored deep. *Pity he wasn't as good with wives.*

Correction: *with her.* He'd been an adoring, devoted husband to his first wife. But then he'd doted on Jasmin, everyone said so.

Samira's hand curled around the door jamb as anguish sucked the air from her lungs and swiped the strength from her knees.

Weeks ago in hospital, she'd mistaken Tariq's delight in their baby for something else. She'd believed he cared for *her* in the way she craved. But she'd been horribly mistaken.

It was as if those moments of intimacy had never been.

She pressed the heel of her hand to the tearing ache in her chest. Yet nothing could stop the grief ripping her apart.

Terrible as it had been before Layla's birth to know Tariq didn't love her, she'd found the strength to bear it. But now, after her luminous joy in the hospital when she'd been so *sure* he cared, the awful, polite emptiness of their marriage was destroying her.

Samira couldn't take much more. Even her bones felt brittle with the effort of holding herself together on the outside when on the inside she was a shattered, bleeding mess.

She'd given her heart to Tariq but he wasn't interested. What she'd thought was genuine tenderness in the hospital had been a mirage, an illusion brought on by exhaustion and wishful thinking.

All her life she'd known the dreadful danger of 'love'. She thought she'd plumbed the depths when Jackson had betrayed her and that, as a result, she'd immunised herself against its power. Only now she realised what she'd felt for her faithless lover was nothing in comparison to this soul-wrenching love for her husband.

She must have made some sound of distress for Tariq swung around.

Her heart dipped as she read the familiar signs when he saw her—the instant stiffening of his shoulders, the guarded expression, the distance he somehow put between them even without physically moving.

Samira grabbed harder at the door jamb.

'Hello, Tariq.' Her voice was husky but firm and she jutted her chin higher.

'Samira, shouldn't you be resting?'

Her mouth twisted mirthlessly. She was always being told to rest when she wanted to be with him.

'I want to see my baby. Between you and the staff I barely get any time with her.' Bitterness made her exaggerate. She wanted to lash out at Tariq, sick of this distant politeness that was all they shared now.

She breathed deep, seeking calm.

For so long she'd craved a child, believing it would fill the stark emptiness within. And it was true; Layla was the light of her life. The tenderness she felt whenever she looked at her daughter had no comparison.

But too late Samira had realised a baby couldn't make

her whole. Only she could do that, except she'd made the mistake of giving away a vital part of herself to Tariq. The man who'd never be the husband she wanted because he was still in love with his dead wife. The man who viewed her not with love but as a responsibility.

Shoring up her strength, she walked into the room, not even flinching at the careful way Tariq passed their baby over so as not to touch Samira.

She compressed her lips, biting down the reproach that hovered on her tongue.

What was the point in berating him? He couldn't help what he felt. In other circumstances she'd be full of admiration for a man so loyal to his one true love.

Something wrenched deep inside and she turned away, blinking back hot tears as Layla nuzzled at her breast. Love for her little girl filled her, yet even that couldn't bring peace.

She was trapped in a web of her own devising.

'Goodnight, Tariq.' She didn't look at him. Slowly, her body cramped with a soul-deep ache, she settled in the low chair by the crib and undid the belt of her robe.

Tariq's hands clenched as he watched Layla suckle at her mother's breast. He never tired of the sight, despite the raw discomfort it brought him. Who'd have believed watching a woman feed a baby would be so arousing?

Not just any woman but Samira.

Even with dark circles under her eyes and her skin pale with tiredness, his wife made him hard with wanting. More, she twisted his gut in knots.

He tried to do the right thing, to keep some physical distance while she recuperated from childbirth. Just remembering that labour made his belly churn.

It had been excruciating torture, watching Samira suffer, and pretending to a confidence that all would be well when at the forefront of his mind was the memory of Jasmin's lifeless face after her emergency delivery.

Even now, weeks after Layla's birth, he woke in a sweat most nights from nightmares where Samira didn't survive. Where nothing the doctors did could save her, because Tariq hadn't got her to the hospital soon enough.

The image of her when he'd burst into the bathroom and found her in labour still haunted him. She'd looked so *vulnerable*. If he'd needed anything to shore up his resolve to keep his distance until the doctor said intimacy was safe, it was that.

'You're still here?' Samira looked up, a frown on her delicate features.

He stiffened. 'It's late. There's nowhere else I need to be.'

She opened her mouth as if to speak, then turned instead to watch Layla.

As if he wasn't there.

Tariq scowled. He wasn't used to being dismissed. Even if his self-imposed rule was to avoid being alone with her so as not to be tempted into doing something he shouldn't.

This was different. This was Samira withdrawing from *him*. Not physically, but mentally. She'd been like this since the hospital.

Tariq hated it. Every instinct clamoured that this wasn't right.

He'd told himself after the baby was born they'd resume the relationship they'd had before. Surely he'd imagined the love he'd seen in her face months earlier? For she'd shown no evidence of it since. If anything, her partiality for Roussel's company, never enough to provoke gossip, but still marked, seemed to indicate he'd been mistaken about that.

Yet, right from that first day home from the hospital, things had gone wrong. Tariq had excused himself to let Samira rest, finding one reason after another to keep away. When he'd finally returned, timing his appearance with that of the twins and their nanny, there'd been no welcome in Samira's eyes. She'd looked bruised with fatigue and there was an unfamiliar blankness in her expression as she'd listened to his excuses about catching up with work. As if she just didn't care.

That had shocked him. Though they'd grown apart before the birth, he'd always felt Samira *cared* for him. Her indifference was a blow he couldn't shrug off. It bothered him more than he'd thought possible.

He'd refrained from pressing her, understanding she needed time to recuperate; making excuses, knowing she must be exhausted from labour. He'd found more and more work to occupy him, giving her the space she needed.

But it wasn't working. Something was horribly wrong.

The spark had gone out of her, the vibrant energy that was an essential part of Samira. Her eyes no longer tracked him across the room and he hadn't seen her smile in weeks.

His belly hollowed. He missed that. Missed the way her eyes used to light up when she saw him; how she'd lower those long, lustrous eyelashes to screen her expression when she realised he'd noticed her hungry stare. How her pulse had fluttered faster when he took her hand, even when they were in a receiving line at a royal function.

Nor had he missed the way she called Layla *her* baby, not *theirs*.

Cold crept along his spine. The gap between them yawned wider each passing day. It was no longer something he could control.

She'd always wanted a child. Now she had one of her own. Was that why she shut him out?

Were he and the twins superfluous?

Tariq's heart hammered against his ribs. The chill along his backbone turned to a glacial freeze, stiffening every muscle and seizing his lungs.

It couldn't be. It was just weariness from the birth. The

doctor had advised time and patience. Maybe a change of scenery to lift her spirits. Tariq had planned a visit to the small palace where they'd honeymooned, as soon as he could get away.

'I've been thinking.' He stepped closer and Samira half-turned her head but didn't meet his eyes.

That epitomised all that was wrong between them. Tariq couldn't seem to reach her any more. It wasn't anger that ate at him but concern that maybe this was something he couldn't put right.

Blanking out the idea, he stepped in front of Samira, willing her to look up.

'Yes?' Once more her gaze skated towards his face but never settled.

With infinite effort he managed not to sound gruff. 'A change of scenery might be welcome. A little break away.'

Instantly Samira's gaze meshed with his and he felt the impact of that stare right to the soles of his feet. At last! It was the closest they'd come to connecting since the night the baby had been born. Then she'd looked at him with such softness in her eyes, he'd felt like a god among men.

Yet now for the first time he had no inkling what she felt. The realisation pulled his flesh tight as the hairs at his nape stood on end. Never, in all the years he'd known her, had Samira been so unreadable, so blank. It was as if a light had been switched off inside her.

Fear clutched greedily at his innards. He felt like something precious had slipped away from him.

'You must be a mind reader.' Her voice was low and husky, as if from a tight throat. 'I was thinking the same thing.'

'Excellent.'

But before he could explain his plans she spoke again. 'I need to go to Paris.'

'Paris?' He stiffened.

She nodded and once more her gaze slid away. He wanted to grab her by the chin and force her to look him in the eye. Then he glanced down at Layla, still feeding at her breast, and pulled himself up.

'Yes. Next week.'

'You want to go to Paris?' Why there?

'Yes.' Her voice had that husky quality that always ignited his libido.

Perhaps he'd panicked needlessly. If Samira fancied a trip to the city women equated with romance, how could he object?

Relief fizzed in his blood. The doctor had been right. She was just tired. Tariq would see to it her stay in the French capital was memorable. His mind raced with possibilities.

'That's an excellent idea. Not next week, though. I'll still be tied up in negotiations. But in another week or two I can manage it.'

Satisfaction filled him. Everything was going to be okay. His mouth hitched in an approving smile.

'No. I'll go next week.' There was no answering smile. If anything, her expression was sombre.

'I'm sorry, Samira. That's not possible. You know how important this treaty is. I'm doing the best I can to speed things up but I'm needed here.'

She shrugged. 'Layla and I can go without you.'

For the first time in his life Tariq experienced the sensation that the floor had dropped away beneath him. He almost stumbled where he stood.

'You can't be serious!'

'Of course I'm serious.' She tilted her head, as if curious at his reaction.

What did she see on his face? Outrage? Anger? Fear? For fear was what billowed up in waves from the pit of his stomach. Fear as strong as he'd felt when he'd thought he might lose her in childbirth.

He was losing Samira. She'd drifted away from him and he had no idea how to grab her back.

His palms itched with the need to haul her close, imprison her against him and not release her. But that wouldn't work. She was with him now physically, but mentally, emotionally, she was in some other place. Some place he couldn't reach.

Never had the emotional minefield of the female psyche been so unfathomable.

What did she want from him?

How could he get back what they'd lost?

The metallic tang of alarm filled his mouth. Samira in Paris without him? In the city where Nicolas Roussel lived since his contract had finished?

Tariq tried to banish jealousy, telling himself Samira had more class than to betray him.

Yet the idea of Samira and Layla alone, apart from him and the twins, filled him with cold, draining dread.

He shook his head, biting down a terse refusal. It was on the tip of his tongue to forbid her but he knew, whatever his rights as Samira's husband, that wasn't the way to win her over. Brute force wouldn't work, no matter how tempting.

He'd never felt at such a loss.

'It makes more sense to wait.' He dredged up a shadow of a smile that threatened to crack the taut flesh of his face. 'In two weeks I'll have this wrapped up, I promise.' He'd do whatever it took to conclude the treaty in record time. 'Then we can all go together.'

But she was already shaking her head. 'There's no need. I know you're tied up here.'

Something flickered in her expression and Tariq's eyes narrowed. Had she deliberately proposed the visit at a time she knew he couldn't get away?

'Besides, I've already promised—'

'Promised whom?' Nothing could disguise the raw edge of anger in his words. Who was she meeting? If it was…

'That French cabinet minister.' Samira stared up at him with rounded eyes. 'She contacted me months ago about a designing a dress for her wedding.'

'You don't do wedding dresses.'

She shrugged. 'It's not a conventional bridal dress. It's her second marriage and she wants something different. I promised when she was here and I'm running out of time.'

Tariq wanted to bellow that he didn't give a damn about what sort of dress a foreign politician wanted. He didn't give a damn about anything but having Samira look at him the way she used to. To feel the sunshine of her smile as she laughed with him and the boys or lay in his arms, sated and content.

Samira disengaged the now drowsy Layla, revealing one lush breast, its raspberry nipple glistening, and a jolt of need jabbed direct to Tariq's belly. His hunger for her was so predictable, so strong, he'd given up trying to fight it. But it was nothing compared with his need for that intangible connection between them that had disappeared like rainwater on desert sand.

Swiftly Samira covered herself and lifted Layla to her shoulder.

The sight of them together, mother and child, smashed open something hard and tight in his chest. He could almost feel the blood cascade from the unseen wound as he faced the possibility Samira had given up on their marriage.

'Don't worry, Tariq. We'll be fine in Paris.' Samira's smile was perfunctory. 'Layla's nanny will take care of her while I'm busy.'

'How long will it take?'

She shrugged and looked down at their baby. 'A few days, a week. But you're right. A change of scenery will be good. I think I'll stay on for a while. There's no rush for me to return, is there?'

Every sinew and muscle strained as Tariq held himself back, forcing himself not to shout that there was every reason for her to return. That she wouldn't be permitted to leave the country. Her place was here with him and their boys. He had no intention of letting either her or their daughter leave.

Pain radiated along his jaw from his gritted teeth. But it was nothing to the tearing stab of frustration and fury he felt as he fought for control.

He told himself he was a civilised man, a husband who understood a wife might need space and understanding after childbirth.

He would find a way to keep her. He had to. In the meantime…

'Very well. Since you've promised the woman, you'd better see her. I'll have my staff organise your visit.'

Yet, even though he knew he was doing the sensible thing, the civilised thing, though he knew she'd have the best care from hand-picked staff, his gut knotted.

He turned and strode from the room before he could give in to the impulse to snatch his wife up, sling her over his shoulder and secrete her in the ancient harem where stout doors and old-fashioned padlocks would keep her just where he needed her.

Walking away, giving her the breathing space she needed, was the hardest thing he'd ever done.

CHAPTER FOURTEEN

SAMIRA PUSHED THE pram along the bank of the Seine, watching the golden lights come on as the sky darkened. A cruise boat went by filled with tourists. Laughter floated across the water and her steps faltered as she remembered Tariq's deep, inviting chuckle as he relaxed with her and the boys.

She dragged in an uneven breath. She missed the boys, even after just a day away.

And she missed Tariq.

How stupid was that when she saw him so rarely? When they led separate lives?

Yet there was no escaping the truth, even here in Paris. She was in love with her husband. As for clearing her head and finding a solution by getting away from him, that had been an abysmal failure.

All her trip to France had achieved was to make her homesick. She wanted to be back in Al Sarath.

How telling that her adopted country felt like home now. Because the people she loved most were there.

But what would she return to? A rapturous welcome from the twins and polite indifference from Tariq.

She had two options. Go back to the palace and live a life devoted to her children and her work. She'd pretend her heart wasn't broken but it would be torture being so close to the man she could never have. Or take Layla and leave Tariq and the boys. It would be the scandal of the century. Worse, she'd never be allowed to see Adil and Risay again. Or Tariq.

Both options were untenable.

Yet what other choice did she have?

She looked up to see a couple entwined together in the shadows of the embankment. Abruptly she stopped, her heart slamming against her ribs. Her breath snatched as heat pricked her eyes. Searing emotion blocked her throat as she remembered Tariq holding her like that. As if he'd never let her go.

How much she wanted from him!

Too much. She hunched over the pram, pain stabbing low and fierce.

Out of her peripheral vision she caught a shadow of movement, one of her discreet security detail making sure she was all right. Yet another reminder of Tariq.

As if she didn't already have that. Slowly she straightened and glanced down at her daughter's sleeping face. Layla's dainty rosebud lips were such a contrast to the determined little chin she'd got from her father. A tremor racked Samira, starting high in her chest and radiating out to weaken her limbs.

It didn't matter what she did or where she went, she couldn't escape her feelings for Tariq. She'd been appallingly naive, proposing marriage to a man whom, she realised too late, she'd been half in love with all her life. She'd been worse than naive in falling for his 'sex without emotion' idea. With her past she should have protected herself better. Now it was too late.

The breeze along the river picked up and she shivered. It was time she got Layla back to the hotel. Past time she came to some conclusion about the future.

Shoulders slumped, she forced herself to walk on.

Samira had just passed Layla to her nanny for a bath and turned towards her own room when a door on the far side of the suite's opulent sitting room opened.

'Tariq?'

Samira's hand went to her throat as a familiar form filled the doorway. Her chest squeezed around a heart that thumped an arrhythmic beat.

She blinked, unable to believe her eyes. But there was no mistaking that broad-shouldered frame, or that proud visage. Elation filled her. Until she remembered this couldn't be the reunion she craved.

Yet, despite the stern voice telling her to be calm, she couldn't repress the sheer joy of seeing Tariq again.

His face was taut and unrevealing but his eyes glittered like gemstones and his thick hair stood up as if he'd run his fingers through it.

She frowned. 'What's wrong? Is it the boys?' She was halfway across the room in an instant.

'The boys are with Sofia, settling down for a story. I promised you'd see them before they slept.'

Samira lurched to a halt, relief slamming into her, stopping her headlong progress.

'They're here?' Automatically she looked past him. 'You've brought the boys?'

He nodded, his expression terse.

'What about the treaty? You shouldn't be here.' Tariq was a vital part of the negotiations that everyone hoped would bring stability to their region.

'Tariq? What's happened?' The talks had been going well. Surely they hadn't fallen in a heap after all the hard work he'd put into them?

'Nothing's happened.' He stepped away from the door, snicking it shut behind him. His presence filled the room, making her ridiculously light-headed.

'But you had back-to-back meetings all week.' Confusion filled her, made worse by the unfamiliar look on Tariq's face. He looked sombre, grim even, but with an edge of something else, something stark that made her skin prickle. Now he was closer, she saw the bleak look in his eyes.

'Nothing's happened to Asim or Jacqui, has it?'

Instantly he shook his head, closing the gap between them with his long stride. 'They're fine. They send their love.' His hands engulfed hers and to her amazement Samira felt the tiniest hint of a tremor in them.

'Tariq, you're frightening me.'

'Frightening *you*?' He shook his head, the action so minute she wondered if she'd really seen it. 'I didn't mean to.' He drew a slow breath and his massive chest rose. 'There's been no accident, no tragedy. Everything's fine.'

Except it wasn't. Everything in Samira warned that things were far from right when Tariq, the strongest, most self-assured man she knew, looked as if he'd been knocked off-centre. It wasn't just the rumpled hair and raw emotion in his eyes. It was his quickened breathing, the grooves of pain around his mouth, the tension in his broad neck and over-tight grip.

'I think I'd like to sit.' She didn't really want to. She wanted him to pull her into his arms and never let her go. But she couldn't admit to that.

'Come.' He drew her over to a wide sofa with a magnificent view over Parisian rooftops to the glittering Eiffel Tower.

Samira didn't spare the view a glance, too intent on the feel of her husband's hard, powerful hands holding hers as if they were fragile flowers. How long since he'd touched her?

She knew the answer instantly. In the hospital, when he'd kissed her. It seemed a lifetime ago. A lifetime since she'd known hope.

Now she read unease in the lowering angle of his brows and the way his gaze didn't settle but kept moving, flicking across her features and back again. It scared her.

'You've met with your client?' he asked before she could question him.

'This morning. It went well.' For the first time in her life Samira felt no upsurge of creative energy at the prospect of designing something beautiful. Not even a thrill at extending her talents with the challenge of designing a wedding dress. For years her work had been a refuge and a solace. Today, though, it had been hard to summon the enthusiasm she needed to satisfy her client.

'Good.' His nod was abrupt. 'That's good.'

He fell into silence and Samira watched him swallow, the movement jerky, as if something blocked his throat. Suddenly realisation hit.

'It's you, isn't it? Something's happened to you.' Her fingers curled hard around his, trying to draw strength from his familiar heat. 'What is it, Tariq?' Her mind flew from one awful prognosis to another. Was he suffering some dire illness? Her heart plunged. She tasted the rust tang of blood as she bit down hard on her lip.

'You can't leave.'

'Sorry?' Samira gaped up into blazing eyes that captured hers with their searing intensity.

'You have to stay.'

'I don't understand. What are you talking about?'

'This.' With a lift of the chin he indicated the presidential suite and the city of Paris beyond. 'I can't let you go. I need you with me.'

Samira watched his eyes darken to a shadowed moss green, felt the sizzle of response deep inside as he claimed her for himself and couldn't repress a spark of triumph.

How masochistic could she get? It wasn't her he wanted, just what she represented—a hostess, a consort, a mother for his children. A chattel.

'Tariq?' Her voice was a thin stretch of sound as she struggled to contain her emotions. Suddenly she was shaking all over, her hands palsied in his hold, her chin wobbling.

Appalled, Tariq saw the change in Samira. He'd wanted for so long to smash through her barriers, to see again some life and emotion in her. Now he did, but she looked like she was breaking under the strain.

Yet he hung on tight. He wasn't releasing her again.

It was selfish of him.

It was needy.

And he wasn't budging.

'You're mine, Samira. You belong with me.' Her hands lay limp in his. 'Samira! Say something.'

'What do you want me to say?' She sounded impossibly weary. 'You don't deserve the scandal that would come if I walked out on you.' His heart all but stopped at her admission she'd thought of deserting him permanently. 'But I can't live under the same roof with you again.'

There. She'd said it. His worst nightmare had come to pass.

Terror grabbed greedily at him, digging its talons right down to the bone. Pain eviscerated him.

He opened his mouth to speak but no sound came. After what seemed a lifetime he found his voice. It was brittle with self-mockery. 'And I once believed you loved me.'

Samira's indrawn breath hissed in the silence. 'Neither of us wanted love, remember?'

Tariq nodded, the irony of his situation hitting full-force. 'We don't always get what we want, though, do we?'

'Tariq?' She leaned forward. 'What are you saying?'

He could have drowned in those serious, honey-brown eyes. He owed her the truth, the whole truth.

'I married you believing I could have everything and give little in return. I could have the sexiest, most beauti-

ful woman as my wife, in my bed. I could have your smiles
and gentle charm and your passion. All I had to do was
sit back and take advantage of my good fortune, no emotional strings attached.'

He drew a shaky breath. 'Until I realised I had it all
completely wrong.' He grimaced at his blind stupidity.
'Thinking you'd fallen in love scared the life out of me.'
His blood had run cold at the idea of another one-sided
love affair. 'I told myself I did the right thing, withdrawing from you.'

Her eyes were huge. 'That's why you gave me the cold
shoulder? Because you thought I was in love with you?
That's why you didn't come to my bed?' Samira's voice
sounded unfamiliar, sharp with pain. Shame filled him.

Tariq looked down at their linked hands, hers so small
in his, yet he was under no illusion that he was the stronger of the pair. He was a hollow sham of the man he'd
thought himself.

He forced himself to meet her frowning stare. 'At first
it was to protect you and the baby. I couldn't let anything
happen to you. I needed to keep you safe and sex...' He
shrugged. 'You'd already had one miscarriage and I knew
how suddenly things could go wrong.'

To Tariq's surprise, Samira's hands tightened on his.
'You were thinking of Jasmin?'

'How could I not? She was fine through her pregnancy,
but at the end...' He shook his head. 'I couldn't take any
chances. And then, when you told me you wanted more,
you wanted *us* together, I panicked.'

'Because you didn't want me falling in love.' Her voice
was flat and barren. He hated the way it sounded and that
he was the reason for that.

'Because I didn't know any better.' He lifted her hands
and pressed his lips to first one, then the other, drawing

in the sweet taste of her, sucking her delicious cinnamon scent deep into his lungs.

He had to find a way to keep her. Even if it meant baring his imperfect soul.

'I didn't know any better *then*. I thought love was a curse. Until it hit me.'

Samira stared up into a face hollowed by pain. For a heady second, she'd hoped he meant he felt love too. But that couldn't be. The desolation in his eyes was too profound.

'Tariq? I think you'd better explain.'

'You married a man who didn't believe he could love.' Familiar pain smote her. 'I know. Jasmin.'

'Yes.' His lips firmed. 'But not the way you think.' His sigh seemed dredged from the depths of his being.

'You don't have to tell me.' Samira didn't think she could bear hearing Tariq rhapsodise about his one true love. Not now when her heart lay cracked and bleeding.

But he wouldn't let her hands go. And the tortured look in his eyes… How could she walk away from him?

'That's one thing I must do, *habibti*—tell you. If nothing else.' Even that casual endearment tugged at her emotions.

He shifted on the sofa, his knees hard against her legs, and Samira forced herself to stay where she was because, whatever ailed Tariq, he needed her for this moment at least.

'I did Jasmin a terrible disservice.' His voice was rough gravel.

'Because you couldn't save her?' Samira had heard enough, now and in Al Sarath, to realise Tariq blamed himself for his first wife's death. 'You did all you could. Everyone says so, even at the hospital. But some things are beyond our power. The medical team did all they could and they're trained for such things.'

Yet there was no lightening of the shadows in his eyes.

'She died because of me. Because I wanted heirs.'

Samira squeezed his hands, unable to bear his anguish.

'She wouldn't have blamed you, Tariq. She loved you.' Samira spoke from the heart, knowing a kindred connection with Jasmin. If the other woman had felt even half of what she, Samira, did, she'd have absolved him.

'She did love me.' His voice was hollow. 'But I didn't love her.'

Samira started. He hadn't loved Jasmin? She felt as if the world revolved too fast, tilting crazily around her.

'Sorry?'

Tariq turned away, but whether he saw the view of Paris out of the window or something else she didn't know.

'I didn't love her. I didn't know how.' He paused. 'I wasn't brought up to love anyone except, of course, my country. My uncle put all his energies into raising me and my cousins to be capable, strong and honest, men who would never shirk from duty or hardship in the right cause.'

'So I gathered.' Samira remembered the stern older man she'd met during one of Tariq's visits to Jazeer. His smile hadn't reached his eyes and, though he'd been polite to the little princess, it was clear he'd been far more interested in the display matches of fencing, wrestling and riding in which his nephew competed.

Tariq's eyes met hers. 'It was an all-male household. Love wasn't a factor in our lives. We were trained in toughness and above all self-sufficiency. So when it came time to marry—'

'You decided on an arranged marriage.' She'd imagined Tariq swept off his feet by love for Jasmin when instead he'd done as generations of sheikhs before him had done and made a dynastic marriage.

'Not quite immediately.' Something flickered in his eyes, something bright and hot. Then he blinked and it was gone. 'But you're right. Jasmin was suitable in every way: charming, well-born, beautiful and…' He paused. 'A genuinely nice woman.'

Samira blinked. *A genuinely nice woman.* That, finally, convinced her Tariq hadn't been in love with his first wife.

Did he think of Samira as a *genuinely nice woman* too? She didn't think she could bear it.

'And she loved you.' Samira's stomach plummeted in a sickening rush as she realised how much she had in common with Jasmin. Both of them had been in love with a man who didn't return their feelings. How had Jasmin borne it?

'Not initially, at least I believed not. I was absolutely honest about my reasons for marriage. I didn't pretend to romance. But as time went by…' He shook his head. 'Jasmin loved me. She didn't hide it, and she never reproached me for not returning her feelings, but I saw the hurt in her eyes.'

His hands tightened on Samira's and she felt the tension in him.

'She was a caring wife, a good queen. I tried to give her what she most wanted. I tried so hard but I just didn't have it in me. I failed her.'

Samira wanted to tell him that falling in love wasn't something you tried to do. It just happened. But that would bring no comfort. Not to him or to her.

They were in the same place now, weren't they? One loved and one didn't. She compressed her lips, holding back the flood of useless words that hovered on her tongue, choking back distress.

Finally she spoke. 'No one can switch love on just because they want to. You did your best. Everyone says you were devoted to her.'

'I tried. But it wasn't anything like what she felt for me.' His eyes snared hers and Samira's heart gave a mighty thump. 'I realised that when I met you again in Paris.'

'When you met *me*?' Confusion filled her. She knew she shouldn't prolong the agony of this conversation but she couldn't wrench herself away.

He loosened his grip on her hands and looked down, watching his long fingers stroke hers, tracing the exquisite solitaire ruby ring that had been his betrothal gift. What was he thinking?

'When I saw you again I felt things I hadn't felt in years. Emotions I'd pushed aside. New feelings too, things that were unfamiliar.'

Samira stared.

He sat up, his gaze mesmerising. 'I'd wanted you years ago, when you were on the verge of womanhood. I wanted you even more when I saw you in Paris. So desperately I couldn't bear the thought of you walking out and proposing to some other man who'd agree to marry you in an instant.'

'You didn't show it.' If anything he'd been cold—disapproving and haughty.

'Didn't I? I hardly knew what I was doing.'

Samira tugged her hands free and surged to her feet, stepping away from him. 'So, you *wanted* me.' She swallowed hard. Nothing had changed. Tariq was a virile man and he wasn't used to being denied. 'But why did you have to *marry* me?'

She choked back a sob of despair. If they hadn't married she wouldn't have fallen in love with him. She wouldn't feel this awful desolation.

Large hands settled on her upper arms. His warmth branded her and she shut her eyes, telling herself she'd pull away in a moment.

'Because I felt more for you, Samira, than I ever have in my life. Because I felt things I couldn't put a name to. Things that made me feel…different.'

His breath feathered her hair, his chest pressing against her shoulders. 'I needed you in my world as I've never needed anyone. I couldn't imagine life without you in it. I didn't just want you in my bed or at my side at banquets and receptions. You were a part of me and I couldn't bear to release you again.'

'Tariq?'

She made to turn but he stopped her, his body close as a shadow, warming her back. His words, his presence, were almost too much to cope with, but nothing in this world would tear her away.

'I wanted you in every way a man can conceivably want a woman, Samira. I'll always want you like that.' His words were pure magic, hypnotising her and evoking tentative joy. 'I love you. I just didn't recognise what it was.'

'You love me?' Her heart seized, then catapulted into life again.

He pressed his lips to her hair in the gentlest caress and her eyelids fluttered as emotion filled her. She had to be dreaming. Yet with his words in her ears, his touch on her body, it felt so *real*.

'I think I came close to loving you all those years ago, though I couldn't put a name to it then. Certainly I planned to marry you, until I heard you were going to study overseas.'

'And that stopped you?' Still she couldn't believe it.

'I felt guilty lusting after a teenager. What right had I to come between you and your dreams? Besides, I needed a wife in Al Sarath, not in Paris or New York.'

'I don't… I can't believe it.' It was too far-fetched. 'You said you couldn't love.'

'All my life I thought so.' His mouth moved against her scalp. 'I didn't realise, you see. I spent so long telling myself that because I couldn't give Jasmin what she wanted. Yet the moment you walked back into my life there was no escaping. It was a *coup de foudre*—a flash of lightning hitting me out of the blue.'

'You never said anything.' Samira struggled to be sensible, not let herself be swept away by the wave of elation rising inside.

Tariq loved her?

'I didn't know what it was.' His lips caressed the side of her neck and she shivered, her resistance cracking. 'I just knew I needed you. When I thought you might love me I was terrified, fearing I'd let you down too. Until you withdrew and it hit me what I'd lost.'

'*You* withdrew from *me*!'

'I was a coward. I'd never felt anything like this. It scared me witless. All these months I've wanted to hold you close and never let you go, but I but didn't dare. I was frantic I might lose you.'

As he'd lost Jasmin. Suddenly she registered that Tariq's big body was shaking.

She spun around. Blazing eyes of darkest tourmaline captured her gaze and his raw emotion blasted her. She felt she looked straight into his soul.

'I love you, Samira. I know I haven't made you happy but give me a second chance. I can't lose you.' His voice was uneven and Samira stared, stunned by such vulnerability in this man who was always calm and in control.

'I don't want to lose you either, Tariq.' It was hard to swallow over the knot in her throat.

'But you left.'

'I couldn't bear the rejection any longer. You'd grown so cold. You never wanted to be with me.'

In a single, swooping movement Tariq wrapped his arms around her and tugged her tight against him. His body was furnace-hot, burning right through the chill that had clamped her. She had to arch her neck to meet his gaze and what she saw there was the most wondrous sight in the world.

Samira never wanted to move. Her hands splayed across

his chest where his heart hammered, its racing beat a match for hers.

'My little love.' His smile was crooked. 'I was trying to give you space because I thought I was making you unhappy. You needed to recover from the birth and—'

'What I needed was you to hold me and never let me go.'

'Really?' Doubt showed in his expression.

'Absolutely.'

'I've still got a lot to learn about…' His shoulders rose expressively.

'About love?' He nodded and Samira breathed deep. 'You think I don't? Love was the one thing I've tried to avoid as long as I can remember. Especially after Jackson.'

Tariq's embrace firmed, pulling her against hard muscle and bone. 'Don't talk about him.'

'It doesn't hurt now.'

'I don't care. I don't want his name on your lips.' In a flash the autocrat was back. She looked up at Tariq's strong face and elation rose.

'Because you're jealous?' It didn't seem possible that a man like Tariq—proud, powerful and so very dear— could be jealous.

'Of course I am.' He paused, watching her intently. 'You haven't told me how you feel, Samira.'

Wasn't it already crystal clear?

'I love you, Tariq.' It felt so good to say it aloud for the first time.

The look on his face made her gulp and something in her chest rose and swelled. Joy overwhelmed her and her eyes glazed.

'You don't look happy about it.' His voice was gruff.

She blinked. 'Don't you know women cry when they're happy?'

'You're happy?' He traced one finger over her cheek

and she sighed at the overwhelming sense of rightness at his touch. 'You really love me?'

'I really, truly love you.'

'And I wuv you.' A tiny arm wrapped around her legs and Samira looked down to see Risay, his hair tumbling over his forehead, his pyjamas askew, with his arms around the pair of them. 'I stay wiv Mummy.'

No little boy had ever looked more adorable with his big brown eyes and wide smile.

'Bringing in the reinforcements to argue your case, Tariq?' she said shakily as he bent to lift their son high off the ground.

Her husband's answering grin ignited that inevitable spark deep inside. 'A good general marshals all his forces to win victory.'

'Is that how you feel—victorious?' She kissed Risay on the cheek and slanted a sideways look at her husband.

He shook his head. 'Not victorious. I don't think I could ever take this for granted.'

He bent and kissed her full on the mouth, ignoring Risay's giggles, and Samira clutched him close, her heart welling with tenderness and awe.

'But I'm the happiest man alive. And I intend to make you the happiest woman.'

EPILOGUE

'SHE'S A DARLING, isn't she?' Samira looked at the delicate features of their little daughter as Tariq placed her in the cot and drew up the sheet. The sight of him, such a big, brawny hunk of a man, so infinitely gentle with the tiny, trusting child made her heart turn over.

He was everything she could ever want in a man and more. Far more.

He turned, pausing when he saw her expression. Then he reached out, drawing her close. Her breath sighed out as he pressed her head to his shoulder and she felt the strong, steady beat of his heart. She slid her arms around him, squeezing tight.

'She *is* a darling.' His voice rumbled up against her ear. 'Just like her mother.'

Samira smiled. After two years of marriage, she was complacent, knowing Tariq always spoke the truth to her now. There was nothing but honesty between them and a deep, abiding love that filled her world to the brim.

Callused fingers tilted her chin up. 'Thank you, *habibti.*'

Her brow knitted as she met his eyes and felt the inevitable snap and sizzle between them.

'What for? I was the one who wanted another baby.'

'And it was a pleasure to let you persuade me.' Heat gleamed in those mesmerising eyes and Samira's breath caught.

'You didn't take much persuading.'

'What can I say?' Tariq smoothed his palms down her back and she arched into him. 'I enjoy your persuasion so much.'

Her heart skipped a beat at the look he gave her. Sometimes she couldn't believe how lucky she was.

'Not every man would agree to adopt.' But she'd had to ask. The little orphaned girl, born in one of the mountain villages and destined for an orphanage, had stolen her heart.

'Then I'm happy not to be every man.' Tariq's words dragged her back to the present. 'Not every man is fortunate enough to marry his soul mate.'

He bent and pressed a gentle kiss to her brow, the tender salute melting her insides, making her cling tight.

'Thank you, my sweet, for your generosity in naming her Jasmin. Not many women would do that.'

Samira shook her head, smiling. Secure in Tariq's love, she no longer felt jealous of his first wife. 'She was a special person. Look at the sons she produced.'

It had been a chance symbolically to lay the ghost of Tariq's guilt to rest. The shadows had gone from his eyes now that he'd stopped looking back to the past, too focused on the present and his growing family.

'You're a woman in a million, Samira.' He cupped her face and brushed his firm lips across hers, stealing her breath.

'I'm glad you think so.'

'Oh, I know so.' Something glittered in his eyes and Samira had no trouble identifying it now.

Love. Love that he didn't bother to mask.

As ever, her pulse pounded in response, joy making her mouth curve in a smile that came straight from her soul.

An instant later he'd scooped her up in his arms, holding her high against his chest as he strode out the door and back through their suite.

He didn't stop in the sitting room where his official files and her latest sketches awaited them. Instead he kept going into the bedroom.

'Tariq! You told me you had work you wanted to finish tonight.'

He stopped at the foot of the wide bed, slanting a knowing look her way. Instantly heat eddied deep inside.

'It can wait,' he growled, his gaze tracking over her body. 'Besides, I'm being a supportive husband, showing an interest in my wife's career.' His mouth kicked up at one side in a hungry smile that made her breath hitch. 'Take off that wrap and show me the new nightgown you've designed.'

Samira leaned in and pressed a kiss to the bare skin at his collarbone, tasting the salt tang of his warm flesh, feeling her pulse riot inevitably in response.

'Of course, Your Highness.' She sent him a sultry look that made him groan. 'Your wish is my command.'

* * * * *

MILLS & BOON®
Hardback – April 2015

ROMANCE

0315 GEN STD HB